Please return this book on or before the date shown above. To renew go to www.essex.gov.uk/libraries, ring 0345 603 7628 or go to any Essex library.

Essex County Council

About the author

Den Hedges was born and bred in Hatfield in Hertfordshire. He currently lives in a village just outside of Peterborough with his wife, Jane. He is very family orientated and loves nothing more than nice family time.

The Gatekeeper and the Hoogle was an idea he had when at school in 1980, and, although he started the story many times, it was never completed. He made a vow that by the time he was fifty-two he would have the book finished, which he did. He loved writing the book and hopes you enjoy reading it.

Remember, the next time you can't find your keys, it may be the Hoogle.

THE GATEKEEPER AND THE HOOGLE

Den Hedges

THE GATEKEEPER AND THE HOOGLE

Vanguard Press

A CIP catalogue record for this title is
available from the British Library.

ISBN 978 1 78465 778 9

*Vanguard Press is an imprint of
Pegasus Elliot MacKenzie Publishers Ltd.*
www.pegasuspublishers.com

First Published in 2020

**Vanguard Press
Sheraton House Castle Park
Cambridge England**

Printed & Bound in Great Britain

Dedication

For Helen Hedges.
My mum and inspiration.

Chapter One

The bell finally rang.

David Edwards was just one of thirty-two children to shut his jotter and textbook with glee, quickly gathering all his things and shoving them into his backpack. Double maths on a Friday afternoon seemed like a special kind of torture dreamt up to ensure that no one started enjoying his or her weekend until the very last minute.

"Don't forget your homework everyone," Mr. Blackwell called as the children charged for the door. "You may think you have all the time in the world to complete it, but you don't. It'll fly by. I don't want to see shoddy work done in a last minute panic, and I won't be accepting any excuses."

One or two groans were emitted but most of the pupils were paying their teacher no attention whatsoever, having already found their friends and now engrossed in talking excitedly, making plans for their upcoming days and nights of freedom. As soon as that final bell rang, their time was their own and Mr. Blackwell had no further hold over them. This was more so the case today as it wasn't simply an ordinary weekend. It was the beginning of the October holidays.

David made his way out of the classroom door, being crushed with the rest of the children as they all tried to escape at once. Finding a place in the corridor where he could stand without being bumped into, he turned and waited for Billie.

She finally made it out, grinning at him widely. "Two whole weeks of freedom," she said, giving a little skip and a whoop of joy as she reached him. "Time just for us."

"Did you know this wasn't originally a holiday as such?" David said as they began to walk down the emptying corridor together. "The Autumn break began when the UK still had a strong agricultural industry. Children were basically excused from school to be used to help with harvesting crops, potatoes in particular. It was backbreaking work."

Billie stared at him and then let out a laugh. "That's slave labour! Where do you get all this stuff anyway?"

"I read." David flushed slightly. Billie often teased him over the weird and wonderful facts he came out with on a regular basis.

"I know you read," she said, giving him a playful punch on the arm. "I think you spend far too much time up in your room with stuffy old library books. I absolutely refuse to let you spend this holiday that way. I want to do lots of things!"

"Like what?"

"Hmmm, let me see. I want to go swimming at the local pool. I want to go skateboarding. I want to go for long walks and climb trees. I want to go to the shopping centre and look around the shops, maybe play the drum kit in the music shop, or try on clothes that I can't afford to buy, then go for a burger and milkshake at the food court. I want—"

"Slow down, you're making me feel exhausted just thinking about it, and if you think you're dragging me around the shopping centre looking at girls' clothes, you can think again."

"We'll look at boys' stuff too, I promise." She gave him a nudge this time. "Maybe I can give you some tips and hints and you can look a bit cooler by the end of the holidays."

"I don't want to look cool," he muttered. "I just want to look like me."

Billie's face turned serious. "You do know that's part of the problem, don't you?"

David shook his head. "No…I mean…yes, but I don't care. I dress how I want, not how other people think I should. I know I'm not popular, that other people think I'm a nerd or a geek, but I can choose whether I want to be what I am or try to change myself just to be popular. I choose to be me. If that means I'm alone a lot of the time, or only have one or two special friends compared to a lot of casual friends who don't really know me that well, or don't understand me at all, well, it sounds like the better option to me. It's the way I want it, and the way I like it."

"If you say so," she said, looking doubtful for a moment. Then she smiled again. "Am I one of those special friends?"

"You are *the* special friend," he assured her, returning her grin as her happy mood was restored.

"But first, before we do any of the other stuff, we've got something else to look forward to, haven't we? Are you excited?"

David dropped his head and scuffed his feet, his smile fading. "I'm not sure."

"Oh, come off it, turning thirteen is huge. You're going to be a teenager. You have to be excited."

"Not really," he said with a shrug. "It's just a number."

"David Edwards, it's so much more than that and you know it!"

He raised his head and turned to face her. "What, like some big rite of passage, the day the boy becomes a man and all that stuff?"

"Well, why not?" It was accompanied by a huff. She knew he was teasing her.

"Because I'm only turning thirteen, that's why," he said with a chuckle. "I'll be just as much still a kid in two days' time as I am today."

"That's a depressing thought. We've got *years* to go before we have any rights and anyone taking us seriously about anything."

"My point exactly. I rest my case, and I didn't even have to make it. You did it for yourself."

"Okay then, I suppose I have to give in on that one. You have to be looking forward to the party, though?"

David was hesitant, unwilling to say anything negative since so much effort would be put into the event that was happening tomorrow afternoon and carrying on into the evening. It would be a day early, not quite his birthday, but it was the only day that everyone could organise the time to get together. "It's not really a party," he said, unsure of what exactly he would call it instead.

"There will be a gathering of people, there will be singing, there will be the ceremonial carrying of a cake and blowing out of candles, there will be cards and presents, so I would say that definitely makes it a birthday party."

It was David's turn to concede the point. "True. I just meant that it's more of a family get together than the type of party that the others in our class have. They all have parties booked somewhere like a hotel function room or restaurant, with a DJ or band, and all their friends invited."

"Well, I'm coming, so technically all your friends are invited and will be there."

They looked at one another and burst out laughing. David couldn't possibly be offended; it was too true.

Chapter Two

David was showered and dressed in his usual jeans and colourful superhero t-shirt, had towel dried his short, mousy brown hair and combed it into its usual style of a side parting. It didn't need any more attention. He could smell the bacon frying from the kitchen below. He knew there would also be eggs, hash browns, and maybe even sausages too. It was his special birthday treat breakfast, a day early. He might even get another one tomorrow on the proper day, or maybe he wouldn't. He should make the most of this one just in case. Still, despite his tummy rumbling and his mouth watering at the thought of what awaited him, he was reluctant to go downstairs. His family's situation was a bit strange, to say the least.

He'd been absolutely devastated when his parents had sat him down around four years ago and told him they were getting divorced. Of course, the news had been accompanied by all the usual reassurances that it had nothing to do with him, that they both still loved him just as much, his dad would always be a huge part of his life, and that he would see him often. However, David was little then and as far as he was concerned, his world had just fallen apart, no matter how many reassurances they gave him. He was close to his father, and needed the male influence in his life. He often wondered if that had a lot to do with why, two years later, his father had moved back in.

Not that they'd gotten back together or anything, despite him lying in bed every single night and wishing for that to happen, and hoping for it every time he saw one of them smile when they talked. No, no such luck. The new arrangement was strictly as housemates and maybe friends. The more he thought about it the more certain he became that it was simply so that his Dad, William Edwards, could be there more for his son. David couldn't deny that he hadn't been coping well without him around. Putting him first and making sacrifices was exactly the sort of thing his parents would do. He wished he'd seen it and appreciated it more back then but he'd been too wrapped up in himself.

It had been awkward at first. No one really knew how to act around one another, or how much time they should spend with the three of them together. There weren't any rules or guidelines for this sort of thing. In spite of this being done for David's benefit, he'd quickly begun to wonder if this wasn't worse than only seeing his father for a few hours on the weekends. However, over time, things started to settle down. Working together, they found a balance, trial and error helping them figure out the best way to utilise the large, Victorian, detached house to avoid having to run into one another too often if they didn't want to. Finally, the passage of time made it all feel much more normal to them and they began to feel comfortable and happy with how things were.

Then his mother, Jill, had announced she was seeing someone else.

It had upset the apple cart for a while. Strangely enough, David had a harder time coming to terms with it than his Dad had, but he got there in the end

David had been unsure of the tall, chubby man at first. He hadn't liked him being around the house or anywhere near his mother, monopolising her time and making her look at his big, laughing face with his sandy hair and freckles instead of paying attention to him or Dad. The annoying thing was that his mum's new boyfriend, Andrew Jameson, was actually okay once he'd gotten to know him and as he spent more time with the family, David liked him more and more. He wasn't his dad, of course, but he certainly seemed to go the extra mile to make friends with him. He would spend a lot of time with David, getting to know him, listening to him, seeming to understand him. David grew to really like him, and Andrew seemed to like David just as much in return. He always seemed to show an interest in what David was up to and they played lots of games, watched TV, and did other stuff David liked to do together.

When his mother, Jill, announced that she and Andrew were getting married, David had wondered if it meant his father had to leave again. Surprisingly enough, it hadn't.

He knew he was too young to even begin to understand how this all worked, but his household had suddenly expanded. There was his father, William. Then there was his mother, Jill, and now there was his stepfather, Andrew, too.

It was a set up that took a lot of adjustment from all parties, and one that only served to increase the teasing and bullying at school. That caused David to retreat even further into himself and become even more of a loner. Things only got worse for him in that respect when his father's new girlfriend, Candy Richardson, moved in as well. David's head had spun. He would often find himself practising, trying to get it into his head so that he didn't make a mistake.

"Mum and Andrew, Dad and Candy, Mum and Andrew, Dad and Candy," he would chant to himself, ensuring he never called Andrew Dad or, heaven forbid, called Candy Mum. That would be mortifying. He would also practice their 'couple names' too, just in case he ever needed them. He didn't call his parents by their first names, though, but other adults did, and he was worried about getting confused if they used them while addressing him. In the privacy of his room, he practiced reciting them too. "Jill and Andrew, William and Candy," he would say over and over, drumming them into his memory.

He'd gradually gotten used to it all, but it still felt awkward at times when everyone gathered together, and not only to him. He knew that this breakfast would be one of those times, and he knew things would be even worse when other members of his family started to arrive later in the day. Try as they might, his grandparents, aunts, and uncles really couldn't come to terms with it at all. There were often comments made that made everyone go quiet and stare at the ground. Sometimes they were said by accident and David couldn't really blame anyone for that. He'd spent a lot of time on edge over doing exactly the same thing. Other times, though, they were said deliberately. David didn't like those one little bit, and they were a large part of why he perhaps wasn't looking forward to today as much as he should be, and why he was hanging around in his room instead of running downstairs filled with delight and excitement. Instead, he walked over to his large sash window that overlooked the back garden of the house, leaning on the deep sill to stare out, gather his thoughts, and brace himself for everything that might happen today.

That's exactly what he was doing when he saw it.

To be exact, he'd been staring at his swing, the one his father had made for him. It hung from the strong branches of the ancient oak tree that took pride of place in their back garden, surrounded by lush green lawn. The tree trunk itself stood still and firm as always, standing guard over their house like a dutiful sentry, but the branches and leaves were being rustled and jostled by the typical English breeze. In turn, the swing was doing exactly what it was meant to do—swinging. He'd been watching it for a while, more lost in thought than focusing.

He loved that tree, had hours of happy memories of time spent on its swing, high up in its branches, and even on the lawn beneath it in its shade. What he saw right now was making a memory that would be far from a happy one.

He wasn't even sure what it was he was seeing.

One minute it wasn't there…and the next moment it was.

On his swing.

David peered at it, trying to make out the details of its features, wondering if it was some animal he wasn't familiar with that had escaped from the zoo or something. *That's ridiculous,* he told himself. The nearest zoo is in the city and that's miles and miles away. It wouldn't have made it this far without being spotted and recaptured. *Maybe it belongs to some private collector of exotic creatures that live nearby.* He decided that was ridiculous too. In this slightly snobby neighbourhood in suburbia, there would have been a million complaints if such a person existed, and he would have heard about it long before now. Knowing he had a good knowledge of the majority of the species that lived on Earth, he decided he should be able to identify it if only he could see it better. He grabbed his bird spotting binoculars but found that for some strange reason he couldn't explain, he was almost reluctant to lift them to his eyes. Logic told him he wanted to examine it to determine what it was, but another voice inside whispered that he really didn't want to know. He raised them anyway, his jaw dropping further and further open as he took in what he was seeing.

The thing was a greyish-brown, almost reptilian in nature, yet it had large, round, double-lidded eyes with wolf-like irises that filled the entire space, no white on show. Instead of being amber, yellow, or even icy blue like a wolf, they were bright green, a *really* bright, lime green. The nose was long for the thing's overall size, the jaws large and powerful looking. As he watched, that jaw opened and he could see two long rows of razor sharp teeth and green, snot-like saliva dripping from them and the pointed tongue that flicked around inside the open mouth. The same gloopy green stuff oozed from its wide, flaring nostrils in its crocodile snout. His horror grew as he realised it was standing on its hind legs, balancing itself with a long, thick tail in the manner a kangaroo might, and one of its front legs was holding onto the rope of the swing, as if it were an arm and hand. It was only about eighteen inches tall, but it looked *horrific*. He let out a small shriek and jumped back from the window, dropping the binoculars in the process.

This wasn't possible. A creature like that didn't exist—*couldn't* exist. Maybe he was still asleep and had only dreamt that he'd gotten up this morning. He pinched himself.

"Ouch."

Nope, that wasn't it. He was definitely awake.

He rubbed his eyes and looked around his room, unsure if he was relieved or not that he could see everything clearly and everything was exactly as it should be. *It has to be your imagination.* His inner voice was right. It was the only explanation. Hesitantly, he made his way back over to the window, almost afraid to look outside again. He braced himself.

The thing was still there.

Not only was it still there, it was looking right back at him.

When the mouth opened again and the other leg...*or is it an arm*...lifted up and one long toe...*or is it a finger*...extended out to point at him and the chest heaved up and down, David let out another scream. It could see him, and it looked like it was laughing at him!

He turned and fled, almost tripping over the fallen binoculars, regaining his balance just in time and flying out onto the landing, barrelling down the stairs, all the while screaming for his parents.

Chapter Three

Jill Jameson hurried out of the kitchen, wiping her hands on the apron she had on over one of her favourite and best skirts; a long, flowing one that she liked to wear for only the most special occasions. Her son's birthday celebration definitely fell into that category for Jill. The skirt was paired with a top that was covered in a floral explosion of pinks, oranges, and reds. Her unique style came from her self-proclaimed love of bright, cheerful colours and patterns. Her family often teased her about it, but she would refuse to get annoyed or upset, saying she would never dull down her choices as they made her feel happy. David had to admit that his mum always looked as if she'd made an effort with her appearance, her dark brown, shoulder length hair always styled and looking pretty, her nails always manicured, and her shoes always matching at least one colour in her bright outfits. She never looked harried or flustered like some of the other mums, no matter how much she had to do or deal with. Today was no exception. She looked perfectly groomed as always, but a worried frown was causing her brows to knit together and her forehead to crease. "What on earth's the matter, David? What's happened?"

David raised an arm to point in the general direction of the back garden. "Su…su…su…something's *out* there," he managed to stammer.

Jill knew David wasn't a fanciful boy. He might have a quick mind and a good imagination but he certainly knew reality from fiction, and he was always too serious for practical jokes. In addition to all of that, she could see the genuine terror on his face. She didn't for a moment doubt her son. "Out where, in the garden?"

David nodded, dropping his arm, his eyes still wide and panicked. Jill immediately ran back into the kitchen and through to the dining area, rushing over to the patio doors that looked out over part of the massive back garden. "Did you see it from your bedroom window?"

His reply was whispered. "Yes."

Knowing that she had the same view except for from ground level she peered through the glass, her worry turning to puzzlement. "I can't see anything. What am I looking for and where was it?"

David crept forward, reluctant to come too close to the large windows, trying to stick to the furthest back corners of the room. "I don't know what it was. It wasn't like anything I've seen before or even read about in any book. It was on my swing."

Jill checked again, then turned to David with a smile. "Well, there's nothing there now so you can relax. It was probably the light playing tricks with something normal, a cat most likely, or a squirrel with a mouthful of nuts stocking up for winter."

David shook his head emphatically. "It wasn't. It was..."

He trailed off. Jill smiled at him, waiting expectantly for him to carry on. She watched his mouth open then close, open then close. He was floundering, didn't know what to say to her. "David?"

He shook his head, his expression helpless as he shrugged. "I wish I'd tried to take a photograph so I had proof, but I was so scared it didn't even come to mind. You think I'm being ridiculous, and you'd think it even more if I tried to tell you what I saw."

"I don't think that at all, and you don't need to prove anything to me. I believe there was something there, and I believe that you *think* it was something strange. I just think you're mistaken, that's all. Maybe excitement has pushed logic out for a change, but honestly, there's nothing there now. Come and see for yourself."

He took a deep breath, squared his shoulders, and walked over to the patio doors. He looked out.

There was nothing there. Whatever it had been, it was gone.

He let the breath he'd been holding out slowly, puffing his cheeks. "Maybe it *was* just my mind and eyes playing tricks on me."

Jill could see that he desperately wanted to believe that, but there was still some inner turmoil going on. She was his mother. There was no fooling her. "Want to tell me more about what you thought you saw?"

She had to turn away so she didn't smile as she watched the debate in his head play out on his face. She knew him so well she could almost follow his exact thoughts. She tried to encourage a little more, hoping to make him feel safer. "If you describe it to me I could keep an eye out for it coming back and get a good look at it this time. Then we'd likely see it was nothing odd at all. I could get your father to do the same?"

She watched him think it over, but finally, his shoulders slumped and he let out a deep sigh. "No, you're right. I must be mistaken. I'm sorry. You've got enough to deal with today as it is. Speaking of which, what's that smell?"

They both sniffed and wrinkled their noses. It suddenly dawned on Jill. "Oh my word, the bacon!"

She scurried off to the kitchen area with David following close behind. "Can I do anything to help?"

She showed him the pan she'd quickly removed from the hob. "I think it's beyond any help. It's a bit burnt," she said mournfully.

"That's okay," he said, giving her a smile. "I like it crispy."

Jill knew that wasn't true. He'd never liked his bacon crispy. He was only trying not to make her feel bad because she was putting effort into making his day extra special. He was such a good boy that way, so unselfish.

She wasn't going to point out that she knew the truth, especially when – as if to prove his point – he cheekily picked a rasher of charred bacon out of the pan and took a bite, grinning at her. She couldn't quite hold back her small laugh as she tried to scold him. "David! We don't eat with our fingers out of pans in *this* house. Now your hands will be all greasy. Go and wash them before you get your nice…oh."

She looked him up and down, noticing his choice of clothing for the first time. "Is that what you're wearing for today?"

"Why, what's wrong with it?"

"I just thought that with everyone making so much of an effort to come and see you, you might have wanted to show them you'd put in some effort too."

David sighed. He didn't want to get all dressed up, but he hated to see the disappointment on his mum's face. "All right, I'll change right after breakfast."

She visibly brightened. "Good. Wash your hands then go and sit down and I'll dish up for you."

David did as he was told, then clambered onto one of the high stools at the breakfast bar, the normality of everything pushing away the strange incident this morning. "Aren't we waiting for everyone else, where are they all anyway?"

"Dad and Andrew have already left in separate cars to go and pick everyone up. You know Andrew's parents live quite a long way away, and Dad has a few errands to run for me on the way so he wanted to get going. We were hoping to have breakfast together but you took too long to come downstairs, lazybones. Candy's still upstairs I think, still getting ready no doubt."

"In the bathroom then, in front of the mirror."

"David, be nice!"

Even as she reprimanded him, they shared a knowing look and a small smile. David never really understood why Candy and his Dad were together. Yes, she was really, really pretty – there was no getting away from that as much as he hated to admit it – but she was so much younger than he was, just nineteen whereas his dad had not long ago celebrated his fortieth birthday. Not only that, but she was a real girly girl, all giggly. It drove David to distraction, as did the fact that she didn't seem to have a brain at all, or if she did, she didn't like to use it much. The way she looked seemed to be the only thing that was important to her and she spent hours on her appearance. David had also heard his mum use the term 'displaying her assets' when talking about Candy to one of her friends on the phone. He hadn't heard the phrase before but had given it some thought and decided that it had to be referring to Candy's short skirts and low tops. He sometimes heard the two women in the household arguing over Candy's outfits, his mum using words like inappropriate and revealing. David didn't know about that, but he did know that Candy spent hours in the bathroom every day, radio blaring, singing along as she blow dried and styled her hair, applied her makeup, painted her nails, and did whatever else it was that girls did.

As much as he didn't want to, David couldn't help but notice the results of all the effort she put in and take note of those short skirts and low tops. It was something that seemed to have happened quite recently and was completely out of his control. It had either appeared from nowhere or crept up on him without him noticing, he couldn't tell which, but it was downright embarrassing. He hoped that it would get better and go away, that he could eventually stop staring at those long legs that were so often on display, stop noticing the mass of blonde hair that she loved to flip and play with by twirling it around her fingers, and stop admiring those large, round, baby-blue eyes that she flashed at everyone when she wanted her own way. He told himself frequently that it was what was on the inside that was important, that it was brains that were sexy, and that he preferred girls that weren't so self-obsessed with their appearance; smart, sassy girls like Billie. He couldn't help but smile as he thought of his tomboy friend. She would be more his type of girl, if he was to think of her in that way, which he absolutely didn't. It was just that Candy made everything so...obvious.

If he was being really honest, he didn't really like Candy as a person. Not only did her constant giggling get on his nerves, but she also seemed to follow him around, always hovering and watching him. He couldn't help but notice that since he put so much effort into trying to avoid being around her. It made him uncomfortable—sometimes it even felt downright creepy. He couldn't explain why or put his finger on it, but something just felt off about it, or maybe about her. Anyway, she was part of the family now and everyone just had to put up with that. Any effort he made with her was for his dad's sake. He jumped guiltily as the subject of his thoughts bounced into the room.

"Do I smell burning?" Candy asked.

"Just a little overdone bacon," Jill replied, handing David a piled plate of bacon, scrambled eggs, sausages, and hash browns, his absolute favourite breakfast. "Nothing to worry about. Would you like some?"

Candy glanced at David's plate and giggled. "I would say that's more than overdone, more like cremated. I'd love some but I'm watching my figure so no, thank you. I'll stick to my muesli. I don't know where you're going to put all that, David. You're like a beanpole. You must have hollow legs. Not exactly healthy, though, is it? I'm going to open the patio doors to get rid of that smell."

"No!" David yelled, making her jump. She stared at him. "My breakfast will get cold," he muttered by way of explanation for his reaction.

She shrugged, walked over to the cupboard, and got herself a bowl. "So remind me again of all the people coming today, and their names. You know how bad I am with names and I don't want to offend anyone."

"It's no one you haven't met before. All the grandparents, aunts, uncles, and some of the cousins, and Billie of course," Jill told her.

"All the grandparents means an extra set for you, doesn't it, David? Extra spoiling. Happy birthday, by the way."

She ruffled his hair, making him flinch away from her. "Yeah, thanks, but it's not my birthday yet."

"Don't be such a grouch. Today's the day we're celebrating it so I get to say it as much as I want." She poked her tongue out at him then giggled; the sound grating on his nerves already.

He forced a smile. "Okay then." He couldn't wait for Billie to get here.

Hoping to dissuade Candy from any further conversation, he loaded up his fork and crammed his mouth full of his special treat breakfast.

***

The day was going well. The family had all arrived bearing birthday wishes and laden with piles of gifts. David had felt slightly embarrassed at being the main focus of attention, but also felt shyly pleased that everyone was so keen for him to have a good day and that he'd received so many great presents. He'd almost completely forgotten about the weird sighting he'd had that morning. Everyone was in the living room, feeling sleepy and stuffed full after a huge buffet for lunch, party games all afternoon, and large slices of birthday cake at teatime. Billie sidled up to him and leaned over to whisper in his ear, her black curly hair sticking out in wild spirals and tickling his cheek. "Did you notice I haven't given you your present yet?"

"You gave me a card that you'd written the verse for yourself, what more could I want?" David asked with a grin.

"Aw, sweet, but you didn't really think I wouldn't give you anything else did you?"

"I've been spoiled enough already. I really don't need anything else so if you didn't it's absolutely fine."

"Rubbish. Come through to the kitchen with me. I'd like a little privacy for this. Besides, your dad's girlfriend is getting on my nerves."

"She does that," David agreed. "Come on then."

Within moments, they were standing in front of the large patio doors.

"What's with her anyway?" Billie asked, still not having left the subject of Candy.

"I have no idea. It would depend exactly what about her you're referring to."

"All the giggling and hair flipping, checking the nail polish for chips, and always glancing over at you to see if you're watching. I reckon she fancies you or something."

"Urgh, don't be daft, or creepy," David said, flushing bright red. "She's with my dad, remember."

"Oh, right, that would be a bit creepy then. Forget I said it. I just sometimes forget they're together because she's closer to our age. Anyway, never mind that. Do you want this present or don't you?"

"Yes, please," he replied with enthusiasm.

He knew that whatever Billie had brought, he would love it simply because it was from her.

She stuck her hand into her pocket and pulled out a small square box that had been stuffed there all day. She made a face, trying to fix the small bow on the top that had been squashed. "Sorry about that. The wrapping's torn too."

David couldn't help but laugh. It was so Billie. "I'm just going to rip it anyway, so it doesn't matter."

He took the box from her, eager to remove the sad-looking packaging. He tore it off in one and tossed it onto the casual dining table beside them. In his hand was a small, polished wooden box with a hinged lid. Excitedly he opened it, revealing a key ring that had an ornate and expensive-looking compass dangling from the end of it. "Oh, wow, this is great."

"Do you like it? I mean really like it. It's a proper working compass, not just for decoration."

"I really, really like it," he assured her. "In fact, I love it."

He carefully removed it from the box and held it in his hands as he turned around this way and that, watching the needle jump then immediately spin back to magnetic north. "It's great, Billie. It might come in handy when we're on one of your infamous rambles through the woods."

"You haven't seen the best bit yet. Turn it over."

He did as he was asked. There, on the back, was an inscription. He traced it with his finger. "I'd be lost without you," he read aloud. "Billie, that's so nice."

Billie dropped her head and shuffled her feet, suddenly looking shy. "I'd thought of matching friendship bracelets first, but knew you wouldn't wear one, even though they look really cool on guys. Then I saw these and knew they were perfect. Look."

She reached for the chain that was around her neck and pulled something out from beneath her t-shirt, revealing a matching compass. "They're a set, a pair. It even has the same inscription on the back."

"So we'll always be able to find one another," David said with a huge grin, knowing exactly how his best friend would have interpreted those words when she'd first seen them.

"Exactly."

He stepped forward to give her a hug. It was over quickly, both of them uncomfortable with physical contact that wasn't playful punches or nudges. David stepped back. "I'll put this back in the box and take it through to show everyone. Thanks again, Billie. It really is great."

Just then, something outside caught his eye. Still clutching the compass in his hand, he stepped closer to the patio doors and peered out. It was dark now, impossible to see out with the light on the inside. He cupped his hands against the glass and tried to look through the shield from the reflections he'd created.

"What is it?" Billie asked.

"I thought I saw movement out there."

"You won't see anything that way, silly. You need to put either this light off or the outside lights on. What's the big deal anyway? Probably just a cat or a fox. I've read about urban foxes becoming a real problem in some areas."

"Yes," David murmured, foxes the farthest thing from his mind right now. Seeing movement out back had reminded him of the earlier incident and brought back a twinge of the fear he'd felt this morning.

Billie gave a long-suffering sigh and ran to the utility room, flipping three switches at once. David practically leapt a foot into the air as outside was flooded with bright light from both the security lights and ornamental lights that were positioned around the back lawn. Now he could see out there properly, his breath caught in his throat. Standing in the centre of the lawn and staring right back at him was the creature he'd seen earlier. It too looked startled for a moment, blinking in the sudden bright light, then opening its jaws and grinning at him before darting off into the rhododendrons.

"Is that better," Billie said, back by David's side.

He hadn't noticed her return. "Did you see that?" He asked in a hushed tone.

"See what?"

He turned away from the window and looked her in the eye. "Did you see anything outside?"

"No, nothing. What's going on, you're being weird."

David chewed at his lip. Judging by the moment she'd spoken, she should have been back in time to see the creature just before it ran off. Did that mean she just hadn't looked outside, or did it mean he was going crazy after all? Maybe it was a symptom of some physical illness, a hallucination, or something else caused by some nasty medical condition. If that was the case, then she deserved to know. She was his best friend. "Sit down, Billie. I need to tell you something."

Chapter Four

David laid on his bed, the lamp still on even though he would be in trouble for it if he was caught. There was no chance of sleep anyway and to tell the truth, the thought of turning it off made him a little nervous. It should have been nothing but a happy day, filled with the joy of spending time with so many members of his family and his best friend. Instead, the turn of events had been disturbing.

He might have been able to pass off what he'd seen that morning as nothing but a trick of the light, but not after seeing it for the second time. Then there was the fact that Billie hadn't seen it, even though she'd sworn she'd looked outside immediately after turning on the lights. She'd reminded him that they'd been friends so long she knew his garden almost as well as her own, and stuck to her guns that there was nothing out there that shouldn't have been out there. He knew she was telling the truth, but so was he and that was the problem, he *had* seen something. When he described what he'd seen on both occasions Billie had been incredulous. He'd seen her struggle to believe him, although she'd really wanted to because of their friendship. She'd really tried but failed. She'd been miserable about it too and by way of explanation, had it in her head that he was playing some sort of joke on her. It was the only way to explain something that sounded too incredible and impossible for her to believe. He didn't blame her. If he'd been in her shoes, he definitely would have considered it some sort of story she'd concocted simply for a game to play over the holidays to liven them up. He'd eventually dropped the subject, to her obvious relief.

Then another strange thing had happened. Their conversation over, he went to do what he'd been about to do when he'd seen the movement outside—put his gift from her back into its box so he could go and show it off to his family looking its absolute best.

Only he couldn't find the box.

He was sure he'd laid it on the table next to the discarded wrapping paper, but when he went to get it, it simply wasn't there. They'd hunted high and low, searching the entire dining area and the kitchen too. They'd even checked the bin, although they both knew it was impossible that it would be in there; they hadn't done any tidying up, they were definitely sure of that! They'd searched until Candy had come through with a message from Jill.

"Your mum says you're being rude to your guests leaving them for this length of time. She says you'd better get back through this minute or your presents are going to be confiscated."

David had looked at Billie apologetically.

"It'll turn up eventually," she'd said with a reassuring smile and a shrug.

It still hadn't.

David had intended speaking to his mum or dad later once the party was over. He really wanted to explain what he'd seen and ask them about it. Maybe they would know what it was. However, considering that even Billie was struggling to believe him, he'd changed his mind. If she couldn't do it then no one else would. His parents might come to the same conclusions that had crossed his mind earlier, that it could be some sort of illness causing hallucinations. They would fuss over him – which he didn't want – but more than that, they would worry about him. That was something he definitely didn't want. His mum seemed to have forgotten all about the incident this morning, hadn't mentioned it again, not even when they were alone as she tucked him in and said goodnight. Thinking about it now and weighing it all up, he decided that the smartest and easiest thing to do was not bring it up again either, and not to mention the second sighting.

So here he was, alone with all his racing thoughts, only him believing in the existence of this revolting creature. What could it possibly be?

He suddenly sat up in bed, a terrible thought slamming into his head. What if it hadn't been the same one? What if there were hundreds of them?

***

David felt exhausted the next morning. His night had been entirely sleepless and it showed in the hint of dark circles beneath his eyes. They felt gritty and he rubbed at them tiredly. It took him a moment to remember that today was officially his birthday.

There was a special dinner planned for tonight, just him, Mum, Dad, Andrew, and Candy, but because he'd spent the entire day celebrating with his family yesterday he was free to do whatever he liked today. That meant only one thing for him—spending it with Billie. He decided he would call her right after breakfast. She always had good suggestions on how they'd spend their time.

Once he was ready, he went downstairs and into the kitchen. Everyone else was already there, milling about and waiting for him to show up. Even though it had all been said yesterday, he was greeted with a chorus of happy birthdays as he entered the room. He blushed slightly, all the attention over the last couple of days a little overwhelming for him.

"Thank you," he murmured.

"Table everyone," his mother said. "Breakfast's ready. Candy, be a sweetheart and help me dish up please."

"All right," Candy said with a grin. "If that means I don't have to deal with the dishes later. I spent ages doing this design on my nails and I don't want to chip them."

"In that case, you can dish up on your own," Jill said firmly, going to take a seat at the table and leaving Candy to take over.

She pouted but did as she was asked while the others all took their usual seats. By the time she started carrying filled plates over, the smile was back on her face, especially when she placed David's in front of him and accompanied the action with a wink. "So how does it feel to be a teenager now?"

"I don't feel any different," David replied, looking away quickly and staring down at his plate.

The last thing he wanted was a girl like Candy talking about him being a man now or anything along those lines. It would just be too embarrassing. Especially in front of his family.

It was Andrew that came to the rescue. "So what are your plans for the day? I couldn't help notice a couple of new video games in that pile of presents. Want to hang out and give them a try?"

"Or we could get that cricket set Granddad gave you on the go," his father, William, said.

"Or I could drive you to the shopping centre so you can spend your book tokens," Candy added.

David looked from one to the other, feeling slightly panicked inside. He hadn't anticipated this, hadn't expected them all to want to spend the day with him. He certainly didn't feel like playing video games, that would be full of hidden dangers and maybe make-believe monsters today, he had enough of that to worry about in real life. He also couldn't possibly choose between Dad and Andrew. He wouldn't want to upset or offend either one. He tried to think if he could get everyone doing the same activity. Billie loved sport so would be up for the cricket, but he doubted Andrew would join in. He wasn't that keen on physical exertion, was slightly overweight, and always suggested seated pastimes for them to enjoy. He certainly couldn't see Candy playing cricket either, although his mum was a good sport and would join in with anything. Billie didn't mind video games, but his dad hated them and Mum hated them even more. Besides, he only had two controllers for his console. Going to the shopping centre with Candy was completely out of the question. No doubt, they would run into a gaggle of her giggling friends and they'd all give him pointed looks and whisper about him, making fun of the fact that she was with the little nerd as they called him. She'd probably roll her eyes and pass it off as lame babysitting duty as he stood there awkwardly, feeling small and pathetic. The very thought of it made him shudder. Either that or she would see something pretty or sparkly in a shop window, be distracted by it and abandon him, probably forgetting she'd even brought him.

This was impossible. Try as he might, he couldn't think of anything that would bring them all together and make them all happy, yet there was no way he could choose between them. The only solution seemed to be to stick to his original plan and go somewhere with just his best friend. That way, none of them would feel more slighted than the others. Offending them all equally seemed the fairest option. Besides, he would see them all at the special sit-down dinner his mum had planned for tonight anyway. It would be special because, with all of them having their own schedule and work commitments, eating together was rare. It would just have to be enough to keep them happy. Besides, it was only fair that he spent the day with Billie since she wasn't invited tonight. He was determined, even though he did feel a little sorry for disappointing them. He'd just opened his mouth to find a way to explain when the phone rang.

"I'll get it!"

He leapt from his seat and ran to grab the handset in the kitchen. "Hello?"

He waited in anticipation to hear the voice at the other end. "Good morning, birthday boy. How does it feel to be thirteen?"

"Billie," he said, his voice laden with relief.

He turned to grin at his family, who were all watching to see if the call was for them. His mother nodded to say she'd heard and turned to Andrew, engaging him in conversation. Within seconds, they were all talking amongst themselves and not paying him any attention at all. Still, he lowered his voice when he spoke again, just to be safe. "Save me. Get me out of here."

He heard her laugh at the other end. "That bad? Okay, I had an idea for today anyway. How about going to our treehouse? I thought I could make us a picnic lunch."

David closed his eyes for a second, picturing it. Their treehouse wasn't really what you could call a proper treehouse. It was built about halfway up an easy to climb oak, quite small, makeshift, constructed mostly out of fallen branches and rubbish they'd scoured the woods for and put together the best a couple of kids could. Still, it was so deep in the woods that it was their secret, a hideout, a sanctuary even. They'd spent a lot of time there playing role playing games when they were younger, everything from pirates to kings in castles, then when everything started going wrong in David's family and his life seemed to be falling apart, they just sat there for hours talking, Billie letting him work through it in his own way, far away from prying eyes and listening ears. There in their haven, he could say whatever he wanted, express how he felt, even cry if he had to. The place now looked and felt a little childish to them, but David couldn't think of anything better than spending the day there today.

"Sounds terrific. It'll give us a chance to use our compasses. I'll take pencils and paper and we'll make an up to date map using the real coordinates."

"Using the compasses was exactly what I had in mind too," Billie replied, filled with enthusiasm now that her idea had been approved. "Love the map idea. Give me some time to put the picnic together and pack my backpack. I'll be over in about an hour."

"Can't wait. As soon as you can. I'll be ready and waiting. See you in a bit!"

David hung up and headed for the door. "Sorry, got to rush. I'm going out with Billie and need to get things ready," he called to everyone as he scurried off, not wanting to look back to see if any of them looked disappointed.

***

"There, it's perfect!"

Billie leaned back in satisfaction, admiring her handiwork on the map they'd created together. David had noted all the coordinates and various landmarks, especially the oak where their treehouse was located, and Billie had added her artistic flair to bring it to life with coloured pencils. "It looks just as good as any of the maps we've seen in fantasy books in the library."

David examined it. "It actually does," he agreed. "Good job."

"Joint effort. Hey, you should keep hold of it. Maybe one day you can write the story that should go with it. You read so much it wouldn't surprise me if you wrote your own books one day."

"Oh, I don't know about that. I don't think I've got enough imagination for starters."

Billie looked at him. "What about your creature, couldn't you write about that?"

David's face fell. "No, I wouldn't want to."

She studied him for a moment. "David?"

"Yeah?"

"I've been thinking about what you told me, thinking about it a lot. I really don't know what to make of it if I'm honest. I've looked at it from every different way possible. I didn't sleep a wink last night."

"Me neither," he admitted. "I was doing the same."

She nodded. "That's what I thought. I've come to a conclusion, right here, right now. It doesn't matter if I can believe it or not, the fact is I can see that you believe it, and I believe in *you*, if not the existence of little, green-eyed monsters."

David's heart lifted, then crashed again. He shook his head. "Wait a minute, are you saying you believe me or not? I can't quite tell."

"Neither can I really! What I'm saying is that I'm willing to accept that you see it, and the next time you say something's there, I'll know you can see something even if I can't. I suppose when it comes down to it, what I'm trying to say is that I *do* believe you, although I didn't know that until now."

David was overwhelmed by the level of trust from his friend. "Thank you, Billie. That means so much. When you think you might be going crazy or seeing something from another planet, then it's good to know that someone at least is willing to listen. I think I would go crazy if I couldn't talk to you about this."

"Is that what you think it is? An alien?"

"I don't know. It was one of the things that kept me awake last night. I went through every possibility and couldn't settle on anything. All I know was that it looked scary, and then I had another thought that scared me even more. I can't say for sure it was the same one I saw twice. There might be more than one."

"Hmm, maybe, but it seems unlikely, especially when you saw it in the same place. I wouldn't worry about that. Have you seen it today?"

He shook his head. "No, not even a glimpse."

"Well, there you go then. I checked the news and there weren't any mysterious sightings or animal attacks reported. Maybe it was just something passing through and it's already moved on to wherever it's going, maybe you won't ever see it again, then you can just forget about it."

"I hope so. I really, really hope so."

Chapter Five

David had felt much happier after their chat and had really enjoyed the rest of the day spent with Billie. They'd played in the treehouse the way they used to as if they were kids again. He'd been reluctant to head home when the time had come, but knew he'd be in big trouble if was late. He'd arrived home, washed, changed, and feeling ravenous after all the fresh air and exercise, had sat down with his family to enjoy his birthday dinner.

Now he was relieved that it was almost over.

It had been a slightly uncomfortable affair. Andrew was still sulking since he'd wanted to take everyone out to a fancy restaurant as his treat. In fact, all of them had their own ideas on how David would want to spend his birthday.

Candy had wanted to take everyone to a fast food joint as she'd thought David would enjoy that the most at his age. William had wanted to order a Chinese takeaway and eat it in front of the TV with a movie as it was something they used to do as a family before the divorce, and Jill had wanted to make David's favourite and have it as a sit down meal around the table in the formal dining room that they hardly ever used. It had been argued over for a good couple of weeks in the run up to the big day itself.

Different ideas and opinions were all part of the weird family dynamic David had grown accustomed to, and although he mostly accepted it as pretty normal, sometimes it exasperated him. It had been William who'd finally realised that the only person who hadn't had a say in the matter was David himself. Finally, he was asked what he wanted to do.

Being who he was, he'd chosen the meal at home lovingly prepared by his mum. Nothing else could even compare, although he'd begged for it not to be in the dining room at the dark, highly polished oak table, sitting on the antique Jacobean style chairs with their high, ornately carved backs and minimal padding. The room suffocated him, made him feel as if he shouldn't laugh, shouldn't speak, or shouldn't relax. Not only that, but the seats gave him a numb bum. He'd pleaded his case for the table they nearly always used - the casual, comfortable one in the bright and cheerful dining area across from the kitchen. Everyone except Andrew had gracefully accepted his decision. David had a feeling he knew why.

The two adult men of the house did appear to get along quite well on the surface. They were always amicable to one another when there were others around, but David could sense a slight undercurrent of something running between them, a tension of some sort. He was sure everyone was aware of it but nobody spoke about it, at least not in front of him anyway. It had always been there, and as he'd grown older, he'd decided that it was an element of competition he was sensing, a one-upmanship caused by testosterone that men sometimes couldn't help. He supposed if any situation was to bring that out it would be the one he lived in. He often wondered if that's why his Dad had gone for such a young girlfriend.

Andrew's particular way of trying to provoke William was to show off in other ways. As close as Andrew and David were, David had no clue what Andrew actually did for a living. He knew he left the house at the same time every weekday morning wearing trousers, a shirt, and a tie; his sandy hair overlong and always a little unruly, sometimes even with two or three day stubble on his chin, whereas his dad was always fully suited and booted, his light brown hair always kept short and neat, and always cleanly shaved. Even though he never said what he did, Andrew liked to give the impression that he made much more money than William did, and he took every opportunity to flaunt that fact. Taking them all out to a fancy restaurant, paying the bill with aplomb, and humbly brushing off their thanks would have been right up his street. He'd been thwarted this time, and David was sure that was the reason behind his miffed silence during the meal. Whatever it was, it was creating an atmosphere. David couldn't wait for it to be over so they could all go their separate ways and do their own thing as usual. There was only the dessert to get through. It was bound to be coffee and leftover birthday cake, maybe with some cream or ice cream. The cake was so big they barely made a dent in it yesterday.

He was right. His mother brought it and slices were cut and passed along the line on small, square plates. Gleaming silver dessert forks already waited on the table.

"Oh, by the way, David, that box you said you were looking for?" Jill said as they tucked into layered vanilla and chocolate sponge cake with a thick chocolate coating.

The words 'Happy Birthday, David' had been piped in white chocolate on top and now they all had random squiggles that had made up the lettering on their slices. David was fascinated by them.

He had to work to focus on what his mum was saying. "I found it on the table last night when I was clearing up. I've put it with your other pile of presents in the living room. I hope you'll be taking them all up to your room and putting them away properly tonight. I let you off yesterday because it was so late."

"What table, what do you mean?"

"The table in the dining area of course, where you said you'd left it."

"But I looked there a million times!"

"Not hard enough, obviously. Anyway, it's found and that's all that matters. You'll be able to keep your lovely gift from Billie safe."

"I suppose so," David muttered, not quite convinced that he should let it drop that easily.

He was glad that the box had been found, but the whole thing seemed fishy to him, especially when he combined it with everything else that was going on. He couldn't see how it was connected, it didn't make any logical sense, but he could *feel* that somehow it was, deep down in his gut. He pushed and prodded at his cake with his dessert fork, deep in thought as he tried to catch hold of those feelings and work them out.

Suddenly, something dropped down from the ceiling fan above and landed on the table right in front of him. The thud it made was deep and loud, far heavier than its height suggested, sturdy, strong. An earthy, wet-leaves and bushes type of smell wafted over David, making him think of outdoors and wild things. With his head bowed over his slice of cake, he could see long claws peeking into his field of vision. He raised his eyes but was too afraid to raise his head more than a fraction. As he'd feared, the creature he saw earlier, stood there, its mouth wide and moving in a chatter of laughter. Its face was only an inch or two from his own. He could feel its hot breath on his face, could smell it too—meaty, like a dog that had just eaten.

David froze, his fear paralysing him.

He sat there, mute, every muscle tensed, his fork poised, shoulders hunched. *What are you? What do you want?* He longed to scream the questions out but his throat was closed and his mouth refused to work. It had gone dry and his brain was going numb. It was all he could do to remember that he needed to inhale oxygen in through his nostrils and expel it again.

Then he heard and felt another thud.

Then another.

And another.

Cutlery, glassware, and crockery clinked, clattered, and tinged as it was shaken and rattled on the table. The light above him swayed, the moving shadows making him feel dizzy, his fear making him feel sick.

"Must be a small tremor," William commented.

"Must be," Jill agreed.

How could they be so calm! That was when David realised that if everyone had seen and felt the table shake, then the monsters weren't in his imagination. They weren't a symptom of some horrible, terrible illness like a brain tumour. They weren't a hallucination or a trick of the light. They were real. Very real. And nobody could see them but him. He was completely on his own. No one was going to help. No one was coming to his rescue.

He had to look. Even if he didn't dare, even if it made his heart stop or made him faint dead away, he had to know how many. Slowly, he raised his head.

He could hardly believe his eyes.

The table was crammed full of the creatures, all chattering, huffing, snapping, pushing and shoving for space as more and more landed. Where were they coming from? Why were they here? What were they going to do?

David screamed and leapt from his seat, knocking his chair over as he tried to scramble away from the table full of the stuff of nightmares. He looked around, searching for an escape route, horror rising as he saw the other side of the room. The entire floor, every kitchen unit, every counter top, the top of the fridge freezer, the microwave, even the ceramic hob, was covered in them, all looking at him with keen, sharp, hungry-looking eyes, their jaws dripping ooze and noses leaking snot, some pointing in his direction with those vicious talons.

"David, sweetheart, what on earth's wrong?"

David's head whipped back to the table where his oddball family sat in their places with their cake and silver dessert forks, their crystal glasses and expensive dessert wine, their expressions concerned but calm. Shaking his head, he backed up, causing the creatures on the floor to scatter away from his heels. Walking backwards, he watched as the creatures followed, their eyes never leaving him as they took a step forward for every step he took back. He took it slow and careful just like he'd seen in films, no sudden movements, his breathing deep and low, trying not to show any fear. He held it together until he was about halfway to the door, then he turned and fled.

He barrelled upstairs, along the landing, and into the bathroom where he closed and bolted the door. He leant his back against it, doubled over, breathing hard, a few sobs escaping before he got them under control. Having a sudden thought, he whirled round and checked the room, his knees going weak with relief when he saw it was empty of the foul things. He sat down, his back against the wall, facing the door, his knees tucked up to his chin and his arms hugging his shins. Slowly he began to rock, comforting himself with the soothing motion. He'd no idea how long he stayed there, but it felt as if it was the only safe place in the world right now.

It felt like he stayed in that room for ages, but in reality, it was probably only a few minutes before there was a gentle tapping on the door. He stiffened, imaging one of those ghastly little things tapping on it with one long claw, its eyes bright with excitement as it tracked down and tormented its prey.

"David, darling, it's Mum. Can I come in?"

David closed his eyes, savouring the relief. He heard her try the door handle.

"Can you unlock the door, please? I really need to talk to you."

He clambered to his feet and made his way over, unlocking the door and pulling it open slowly, poised to slam it shut again in a heartbeat. For now, she was alone. He peered behind her, checking that the coast was clear.

"What exactly is it you're looking for, David?"

David looked up into her serious and sympathetic face, seeing that if there ever were a time when she would listen to some crazy, outrageous story of monsters, then it would be now. It was time.

"I can't tell you exactly as I don't know what they are. They're something I've never seen before, something that shouldn't exist." He went on to describe the creature he'd seen, using all the references he could from animals she was familiar with in order to paint the picture for her. He told her of their lime green wolf eyes, the crocodile snout, jaws, and teeth, the scaly body held upright by a kangaroo tail and heavy, powerful thighs, the spindly arms and long claw-like hands with the talons for nails that he couldn't attribute to anything he'd ever seen in any of his nature books. He even described the wild, outdoorsy smell of the things, and the snot that seemed to drip constantly from then.

To his amazement, his mum listened, looking only mildly surprised in some places but otherwise seeming to take it all much more calmly than she should. She ought to be hysterical, panicking, or if not, then worriedly feeling his forehead to see if he had a temperature, calling William, telling him they needed to arrange an appointment with a neurologist, or at the very least laughing, telling him he was being ridiculous. Instead, she simply listened and when he came to a halt, she was all business.

"Where and when did this start and how many have you seen?"

He began at the very beginning with the one he'd seen on his swing from his bedroom window and brought her right up to date with the ones that had invaded the kitchen diner earlier. "They're real; I know they are, even though no one else can see them. What's wrong with me, Mum? Why am I seeing these things?"

Jill sighed. "Come through to your room. We need to have a long talk and we can't be overheard."

David followed her through.

"Sit down and make yourself comfortable," she said, sitting down herself, then patting the bed beside her.

David clambered onto the bed, not too old to appreciate the warmth of her arms as she turned to face him and gave him a quick hug before she began.

"I've got a story to tell you and since you're so interested in science and space you'll recognise parts of it, but it isn't going to be like the things you think you know. There's more to it than you've ever been taught in school or read about in books. In fact, this isn't going to sound scientific at all, it's going to sound a bit loopy, very far-fetched, and maybe even a little bit scary."

Jill had David's rapt attention. His bedroom was offering him some comfort and her presence was bringing a sense of security. He was starting to feel safe and listening to her talk was adding to that, offering him a distraction from what had just happened. He could lose himself in this, and maybe, just for a few precious moments, he could forget all about the monsters. Besides, anything that had to do with science and space was right up his street. He knew his dream of one day becoming an astronaut and travelling through space was probably never going to happen, but it didn't stop him having that dream, no matter if it too was far-fetched and maybe a bit loopy. Not only that but he loved science fiction, and this sounded like it was going to be that kind of story. He couldn't wait to hear it.

"Okay, here goes. You'll have to forgive me if I don't sound scientific enough, but there are parts of this that I never really understood. I'll do my best."

"Fine, just tell me!" David said with enthusiasm

"All right. You know that it's taken as fact and is supposedly documented that several asteroids have hit the Earth since its creation; even though nobody was around to see many of them. When I was around your age, your granddad sat me down and told me all about them. I can almost remember exactly how he put it too. He said that these types of cosmic collisions are fairly typical in the grand scheme of things. It worried me at the time. I couldn't help but imagine walking to school the next day, then all of a sudden this giant rock would come hurtling out of the sky and squash me flat."

Jill gave a little chuckle and shook her head.

"Granddad's right though," David said, "although you were silly to be worried considering the odds of being in the exact spot at the exact time. Did you know a computer simulation has estimated it to have happened around 350 times in the last 10,000 years?"

"I didn't. That's a lot."

David was thoroughly into the subject now, highly excited to be having one of his favourite types of conversation. "Yep, and it can't really be disputed. The evidence is everywhere if we look hard enough; in layers of rocks, fossils, the existence of elements that aren't found on Earth but are abundant in other rocks and planets in space, and even the way gemstones are formed in its core, like that sapphire you're wearing and the diamonds in your eternity ring. Sometimes, though, the effects they leave behind are eradicated over time, the craters disappearing due to weathering, the secrets it might have left behind never ever found. There are ones that we'll never know about, never know where they hit, nor what traces they might have left behind. To us, it's as if they never even happened. Isn't that fascinating?"

"It is," Jill said with a laugh. "I hadn't even given it that much thought. It's funny you should talk about secrets, though."

"Why?"

"Well, you know about the big asteroid, well, I say that. I don't actually know how big it was if I'm honest. The most famous one anyway?"

David grinned. "You bet I do!"

Jill made herself more comfortable, seeing how the tension was leaving his body, the fear leaving his eyes, and the worried, pinched look had already gone from his face. This was doing him the world of good. She wasn't in any rush to remind him of why they were having this conversation, not yet. She wanted to let him enjoy it for a while before she had to bring him back to the world of invisible monsters. She smiled at him. "It was me that was supposed to be telling you a story, but why don't you tell me this one first?"

Since Billie was the only person who would normally listen to him going on about this stuff, he didn't need any further urging. He dived into the telling of it, relating it as if he were narrating one of his beloved documentaries. "There was one particular collision that changed the face of the Earth forever. 65 million years ago, an asteroid struck just off the coast of the Yucatan peninsula. The people who know about these types of things have calculated that it was at least 6 miles wide in size and travelling at 18 miles per *second*—that's 150 times faster than a jet airliner, can you imagine?"

"I can't. It's unimaginably fast."

They shared a laugh before David continued with his interpretation of those historic events, blending together how he'd heard it told by different people, and how he read it several times over written by different scientists and historians. "Anyway, it's said that for months on end, the sun's rays were blocked from the Earth by the huge clouds of thick dust that were created by the impact. Everything went dark and the temperature dropped like a stone. The plant and animal life struggled, some unable to survive, and those that did had a new threat to face. When the dust finally settled – literally, not figuratively – the effect of the greenhouse gases caused the temperature to soar and all the life that had adapted to the cold and dark had to evolve again in a hurry or perish."

"Right, and that's when we lost the dinosaurs, wasn't it?"

"Yep, extinction was rife right across the planet and the dinosaurs were one of the casualties. They just couldn't adapt from the cold and dark to the extreme heat fast enough. It's so sad and I can't help feel sorry for them. Those things were the ultimate predators. They should have ruled forever!"

"What if I told you that there might be places in existence where they do still rule?"

"Impossible," David said. "We've found all the planets in our solar system and there's no way we could have missed a life form on them that big. We haven't even found any signs of life at all, not on any of them."

Jill knew it was time. "David, I'm about to tell you something that's going to sound even more impossible than that to you. I know with your scientific mind and logical way of thinking that you're going to really struggle with this, but I have to tell you and I need you to believe me. I'll mostly be quoting your granddad again as this was his story and he put it far better than I'd be able to. I'm sure he's the one you get all your brains and your love of science from; it certainly isn't me or your father that's for sure."

David was practically exploding with curiosity. "What is it you want to tell me, Mum?"

"Here goes then. What you've said about the asteroid and everything that happened afterwards is correct, only it isn't the whole truth of the matter. There was another effect of this cosmic collision, one that is known to only a small number of people, and none of them are scientists, geologists, historians, or gemmologists. It wouldn't matter what their profession was anyway, as they all have one higher purpose. They are guardians."

David's eyes were like saucers. "Guardians of what?"

"I'll get there. When the asteroid collided it didn't just leave a big old hole, it actually caused the Earth to shatter. Huge chunks of it flew off into time and space and the resultant ripples through those created something unfathomable, especially to those that try to study it from an analytical point of view. The chucks of rock that were pieces of our Earth were all different sizes, some of them small, some of them massive. What they had in common was that they all had life on them in some form or another at the time. Mostly, the life that was on them survived as it didn't take long for the chunks to draw other space matter to them. They collided with other rocks, pulled things in towards them. They grew, they developed, and in the same way that everything on Earth did, the life that was on them adapted and survived."

"No way! Mum, this is a brilliant story. You should be writing books."

"It's not a story, David. I really wish it was."

David could see her utter conviction. He was confused. This was impossible, yet Mum didn't lie, and she certainly never played jokes. She couldn't possibly be telling the truth, could she? Either way, he had to hear more. He hadn't heard about these guardians yet so there was definitely still more to tell. "Go on."

"Evolution of those long lost plants and animals continued as it did on what remained of *this* Earth, each developing in their own way to fit the resources available in their new home. They were all still upon the Earth in a way—only not. Now we're getting to the bit I think you'll really have a hard time over."

"You mean that wasn't it already?"

"No, so listen carefully. Whether it was the suddenness and speed of impact, whether it was the shockwaves that were created by the force throughout space, whether it was the way things were aligned at the exact moment, no one will ever know. What happened that day was that new worlds were created, and yet every one of them was, and still is, linked to this Earth. To this day, all over the world as we know it, there are gateways to and from these new worlds that were created from the fragments of planet Earth. There is little way to tell where they are and even worse, what lies on the other side. It's possible that the majority of us would never even want to know. Some people do know because they have no choice *but* to know. Some people see these gates. Some people can see the worlds beyond, and they see the things that live there. These people are the Gatekeepers."

When Jill came to a halt, David was bursting with a million and one questions. He tried to choose the first carefully. "So let me get this straight in my head. You're saying that all these gates lead to and from different worlds, all like Earth but not quite Earth, but that were originally parts of Earth?"

"That's about it in a nutshell," Jill said with a smile. "I always knew you were smart."

"But wait. If these planets all exist within our galaxy, why haven't they been tracked and recorded like the others, like Saturn, Mars, Neptune? We know quite a lot about them all now."

"I don't know, David. It never made sense to me and I never tried too hard to *make* sense of it. I'm not sure if they *are* close to us in a physical sense, only that the gates make them seem that way. As far as I know, they could be anywhere in space."

David flung himself back against his headboard. "Woooaaah," he exclaimed, shaking his head slowly. "This is absolutely mind blowing. I don't know if I can even get my head around it."

Jill gave him some time, sitting quietly as David struggled with the concept. Finally, he looked less shocked and more excited. "So if all this is true, then there really could be planets out there that still have dinosaurs living on them?"

"There could be, or something like them. Although these new worlds were originally a part of this world, they all developed in their own way. There will always be a few similarities, but also always vast differences. No one really knows what to expect from these worlds. It really isn't a good idea at all to go exploring through them, and it certainly isn't a good idea for anything to be allowed to come through to *this* side either, no matter how exciting you find the idea. That's the first rule you have to learn, and probably the most important one. You should never go through, and you should never let anything come through."

"But I don't understand. Why would I need to hear the rules? Even supposing this is true, why tell me now? Is there a gate nearby; is that it? Are you afraid I'll go through? Or is this something everyone needs to learn when they become a teenager? Is it kept secret until then so they can enjoy their childhood? What are these gates? How can they make something far away in space be close? How do they work?"

"Slow down, one question at a time! There are more gates than you can ever imagine. They're everywhere so it's possible there are ones very near here, but that's not why I'm telling you. I can't answer all your questions, but I can tell you the rest of what I know and it might answer some of it. That is if you're ready to hear it."

"Absolutely," David said enthusiastically.

He'd always loved stories and was particularly enjoying this one. Having Mum here, spending this time with him, sitting on his bed telling him a tale, reminded him of the old days when he was a lot younger, safe, secure, where nothing could ever hurt him. He didn't want it to ever end.

"Okay then. I can't tell you much about the gates; I really don't know how they work. What I do know is that the gates must always remain closed. They must never be opened. We don't know what can come through. Unfortunately, sometimes they do open. They open on their own accord, but there's a very special type of person that can see the gates, and can close them when they open."

"The guardians," David breathed.

"That's right. These guardians are called Gatekeepers, and they're probably the most important people on this planet, although the normal people don't know it. These worlds and gateways are a very carefully guarded secret and you must never speak of them to anyone else, not ever. You know what people are like. They love to explore, they love to discover, they have to find things, examine them, study them, conquer them even. The rush of people who would want to open these gates would be overwhelming if word got out, everyone from top scientists down to the merely curious. The Gatekeepers are a select few. They would be overwhelmed, unable to prevent it, and although you might not realise it yet, you've already seen what type of thing might come through."

Now it was starting to make sense. The creatures he'd seen were the connection, the reason his mum was telling him all this. "You think what I saw were creatures that came through one of these gates, something from another world?"

"I'm almost certain of it, and from your description, I would say they sounded like Hoogles."

"Hoogles," David repeated almost reverently, thinking it was the perfect name to describe the things he'd seen. "Are they very dangerous? They *looked* dangerous."

"Hoogles are more mischievous than dangerous. They like to play tricks. They like to look scary, take great delight in frightening people, but mostly, they're pranksters. You know when you can't find your keys or your phone, the television remote isn't where you left it and you find it down the side of the sofa, maybe even in a place where you weren't even sitting last? That's the Hoogle."

"My box! I knew it was connected somehow but I just couldn't work out how. Was that a Hoogle?"

Jill nodded. "More than likely. It's the kind of joke they like to play."

David was silent for a moment, taking it all in and trying to process all this new information. Now that the little monsters he'd seen had been brought into the equation, it gave credibility to his mum's story. He couldn't see how he could possibly doubt it unless he carried on believing that he was maybe going insane or hallucinating. He didn't think he was anymore. All the pieces fit together like a jigsaw puzzle and explained the strange happenings of the last couple of days. It explained why he couldn't identify the little monsters, where they came from, and why they hadn't harmed him. Then, the more he thought about it, the more he realised the story was raising more questions that it was answering. "Okay, so I get the worlds, I kind of get the vague concept of the gates, and I even get the Hoogles and how they came to be here, but there's still masses I don't get. If this is all such a big secret why do you know about it, and why are you telling me? If the Hoogles are really there after all, why did no one else react to them tonight? Even if they aren't that dangerous, they still aren't something you can ignore, especially not when they're jumping all over the table during dinner!"

"I was getting to that if you'd given me the chance," Jill said. "The reason no one else reacted is because no one else can see them. None of us knew they were there."

David opened his mouth, but Jill held up her hand to silence him. "I know what you're going to ask and I'm asking you to have a little patience. I'm about to explain if you'll let me. The reason I know about the gates and things like the Hoogle is because I know someone very close to me who was one of those chosen few, the special ones."

"A Gatekeeper, you know a Gatekeeper?" he asked in awe.

"Yes, and you know him too, quite well in fact. It's my father, your grandfather."

"Granddad's a Gatekeeper? No way!"

"Yes, way," Jill said with a small smile. "He's one of the people who has lived their lives helping to keep this world a safer place, or at least safe from all the unknown dangers that we have no understanding of and no knowledge of how to handle."

"That's really neat! I can't believe I'm related to one. Are you one too, is that how it works? How do they get chosen?"

"You really don't ever stop asking questions, do you? I can see what your teachers mean now," Jill said, laughing easily now that the worst of this conversation was over. She soon turned serious again, though. "No one really knows how the Gatekeepers were originally chosen, it happened too long ago. If the information exists, it's held as a closely guarded secret. What I do know is that it travels through a bloodline, down through families. Only that the gene is a little like the twin gene. It doesn't always happen, but most of the time, it skips a generation and turns up in the next. It's not me that's the Gatekeeper, David. It's you."

Chapter Six

David was in the middle of yet another sleepless night. He was terribly glad that his thirteenth birthday had fallen at the beginning of the school holidays. He couldn't even begin to imagine how he could sit through classes when not only did he have all these thoughts running through his head, but he wasn't getting a wink of sleep either. He would be sure to nod off if he had to sit through double maths anytime soon.

His mum had gone on to explain that no one could ever tell who would turn out to be Gatekeeper. The pattern that it skipped one generation was fairly common but never taken for granted. Sometimes it skipped two or more, or died out in a family completely. Also, normally, there were no signs whatsoever, not until the potential new Gatekeeper reached their thirteenth birthday. Only after that day did they start to show some indication. His mum couldn't explain to him why he'd seen the Hoogle a day early, or why so many had appeared at once. She'd looked a bit worried about it in actual fact. Still, she'd promised to talk to his grandfather about it. She said they'd likely be visiting him a lot from now on.

She'd explained that now it had been made clear to them who the next Gatekeeper was to be, Granddad Peters would immediately lose all his skills. That was how it happened, and it was always an incredibly vulnerable time. He would have an awful lot to teach David in a very short time.

David couldn't really imagine having to learn any more—his head was fit to burst as it was. It wasn't so much the amount of information as he knew he could remember a lot and that everyone considered him clever, it was more the nature of the information. Gateways, other worlds, fantastical creatures, secrets, maybe even magic; it shattered apart everything he thought he knew, and that's what he was struggling to get his head around and come to terms with. He'd wanted to talk more, wanted to talk about it nonstop if he was honest, but his mum had looked exhausted and he'd eventually stopped asking questions so she could go to bed. Before she had, David had learned that Dad wasn't involved but did know a little about it. He would try to get a chance to talk to him in private tomorrow. Mum had warned him not to talk to anyone else, not even Andrew or Candy.

He longed to call Billie but knew her parents would go spare if he called at this time of night. Still, he couldn't wait to tell her all this! *Mum warned you not to say anything to anyone,* he constantly reminded himself. She'd explained that any knowledge, however small, could put people who weren't part of the Gatekeeper line in great danger. He felt a little guilty now for telling Billie about the creature he'd seen, so much so that he couldn't bring himself to confess to his mum that he'd done it. That would maybe be a little secret of his own he'd have to keep. He knew he could trust Billie not to say anything, and since she knew things already, he couldn't really see the harm in telling her the rest. Besides, she was his best friend. He already knew that this was going to be hard for him to come to terms with and accept. How could he even think about going through it without her, or keeping secrets from her? It was unthinkable. He couldn't leave her in the dark. What if this took up a lot of his time and he couldn't be with her as much as usual? What if he became quiet and withdrawn under the weight of responsibility and she thought there was something wrong between them? No, the only option was to tell her and hope that his mum was being overly cautious in her warning. With those thoughts running around in his head, he finally drifted into a restless and uneasy sleep.

***

When David awoke the next morning, his first thought was that it had all been a dream. There couldn't really be such things as gateways, Gatekeepers, and Hoogles, could there? Or could there? It all seemed so real, his mother sitting on the bed telling him the story, her concern, her affection. It was so vivid and he didn't normally have dreams like those. Normally, if he did dream, he barely remembered in the morning. He closed his eyes again for a moment, thinking it all over. That's when it hit him.

It was all real.

He was a Gatekeeper!

He leapt out of bed and hurried through his routine of showering and dressing, forgetting to comb his hair afterwards. He had so much to learn and Mum had promised he could talk to his grandfather today. As a thirteen-year-old boy, he couldn't help but wonder if the title came with any specific powers. He was already daydreaming about what they might be before he even reached the kitchen.

Much to his disappointment, he found that his mum wasn't alone. Candy was there too, seated at the breakfast bar, eating her special cereal that David had tried once and had thought tasted like cardboard. He couldn't understand how anyone could be so concerned about what they looked like that they would deny themselves anything good at all. *His* breakfast was going to involve something chocolate flavoured and loaded with sugar. Not only did it taste good, he might need the energy in his new capacity. It seemed a great excuse to him. This Gatekeeper thing might just come in handy.

"Good morning," Jill said, already anticipating what he would want and pouring him a bowl of his favourite. "Sleep well?"

"Tossed and turned a little," he replied, knowing his mum would get it without him spelling it out.

"Morning, David," Candy said, joining in the conversation now that she'd swallowed her mouthful of cereal. "You didn't sleep well? Wasn't nightmares, was it?"

Her questions were casual, the tone light and friendly as normal, but she was looking at David and there was something in her eyes, an intense kind of look as if she was far more interested in the answer than she was letting on.

"No, no nightmares, just couldn't get comfortable that's all," he muttered, sliding into his seat.

"Oh, okay, I get it," Candy said with a giggle and accompanying her words with a knowing wink.

David's face flamed, having no idea what she thought she got but feeling embarrassed anyway. It was the *way* she said things sometimes. It made him cringe.

Candy seemed not to notice his discomfort. "So, I was thinking that I could drive you to pick up Billie and I could drop you both at the shopping centre today. Those book tokens and gift vouchers must be burning a hole in your pocket by now."

"That sounds...nice," David said, sounding as doubtful as he felt. All the same thoughts he'd had about going anywhere with Candy the other day still applied, but it wouldn't be so bad if Billie was there with him too. Still, he had other things he wanted to do today, much more important things. He wasn't going to find a book on the topic he was most interested in at the shopping centre. "But I think Mum was going to take me to visit Granddad today, weren't you, Mum?"

Jill smiled. "I think it would be nice to pay your grandparents a visit."

"But you only saw them…like…yesterday!" Candy said. "Surely you'd prefer to spend your holidays hanging out with people more your own age and doing more fun things. What's the fascination with stuffy old grandparents all of a sudden?"

There was that intense stare again, as if she were trying to peer right inside him, see all the way into his head. David swallowed hard then filled his mouth with a spoonful of cereal. "Maybe, it's because they *are* old. Seeing them yesterday made me realise I won't have them forever," he said through his mouthful of chocolaty tastiness.

Jill opened her mouth to admonish him, then catching his look, closed it again. She gave Candy a quick, sideways glance and said nothing. David knew she'd read his thoughts—he didn't want Candy asking any more questions about why he would want to visit Granddad and this was his way of putting her off talking. David's little trick worked.

Candy looked grossed out and curled up her cute little nose. "Well, maybe later then," she said, hurriedly rising from her seat and loading her bowl into the dishwasher before disappearing out of the kitchen.

David grinned at Jill and finished his breakfast in peace.

***

David sat in silence, staring down at the swirly pattern on the carpet, feeling swallowed whole by the large, puffy, chintzy armchair he sat in. On the wooden mantle above the tiled hearth, a clock ticked loudly, the only sound to break the current silence in the room. He'd never felt all that comfortable in his grandparents' small, old-fashioned house—too much of a contrast to the bright, modern interior of his own large one. Today was even worse. Today he was feeling greatly disappointed.

After all his excitement to go see him, the morning with his granddad had turned out to be a bit of a let down as far as he was concerned. He wasn't sure exactly what he'd been expecting, but his granddad hadn't even seemed surprised or excited by the news that he'd seen a Hoogle, or that he was a Gatekeeper like him. He'd taken it as calmly as if David was telling him something perfectly normal—like it was raining or cold out. He hadn't even told him much more than his mother had done last night, more or less repeating the same story over from the beginning, adding very little new, and certainly giving him nothing in the way of further explanation. He sat across from David now, equally as silent.

When he cleared his throat, David looked up at him expectantly, hopefully even. However, his grandfather was still staring into space. David examined him, taking the opportunity to stare.

Geoff Peters was a tall, thin man, not so much skinny but wiry, as if there was great strength in those spindly limbs. His skin was wrinkled, but not plump, powdery, and papery like David's nana's, more weather-beaten and tough looking, like old, tanned leather. From old photographs, David knew his Granddad's hair had once been the same dark brown as his mum's, but now, it was steely grey and just as wiry as his limbs. Even his once bright blue eyes were now pale and icy. Everything about the man looked cold. David wasn't sure if he would say his looks matched his personality. Perhaps cold was a step too far, but he was certainly aloof, often abrupt. David had found him a little frightening and difficult to get along with for most of his childhood. He'd hoped this would perhaps bond them or even if it couldn't go that far, at least give them something to enthuse over together. However, the only time his Grandfather had spoken with any great emotion was when he'd been talking about the amount of gates there were. At that point, he'd turned deadly serious and intense.

"Don't ever underestimate how many there are, David, or how far away from our world they can actually be. No matter how close they seem, or how similar they look, they are worlds apart. If you learn nothing else, then learn that. They aren't safe. They aren't natural. They're an abomination."

Other than that small flash of passion, he'd made the rest of this whole thing sound as if it were no big deal.

Where was the fun in that?

Up until then, David had thought he was on the cusp of a great adventure, something huge. Once he'd learned that the scary-looking Hoogles weren't actually that dangerous, it had become exciting rather than frightening, especially when he thought of all the things he might have to learn. He'd imagined magical chants, superpowers, special ancient weaponry, even phenomenal martial arts skills. Much to his disgust, it didn't seem as if there was going to be any of that. He hadn't even seen any other weird and wonderful creatures, hadn't even seen a Hoogle since his dinner party. He glanced towards the door when he caught the faint sound of laughter coming from his mother and his grandmother in the kitchen. He wished he could go and join them but didn't want to appear rude. He decided to try questioning some more.

"So, Granddad, what's it actually like? Putting all the science and history aside, what does it actually mean to be a Gatekeeper?"

"Different things to different people I suppose."

Blood from a stone, David thought. "Well then, I suppose I'm asking what it actually meant to you."

"For me, it meant never being with your Grandmother enough, always having to be away in places I didn't want to be. It's a massive commitment, but not one that you get to choose or reject. Make sure you're ready for it, David. Make sure your life isn't pulling you in different directions."

David hadn't really understood what he meant. As far as he could see, being a Gatekeeper was the best thing in the world and he couldn't think of a single thing that would be more important, not ever. He moved on, eager to hear some exciting tales of monsters and battles.

"So what else do I need to know? What's the best way for me to learn? Are you going to tell me some stories of gates, or the encounters you had?"

He'd been seriously deflated when his grandfather had stood up, walked over, and patted him on the back, telling him he wasn't going to say anything more for now, that it was enough to take it for one day. It didn't seem like anything at all to David.

Maybe he'd built this whole thing up in his head and made it into something it wasn't. Maybe it was nothing at all, just as his granddad made it sound. He began to change his mind about this having any impact on his life at all, never mind the massive one he'd expected. It seemed as if it would just be a title he carried that would require little effort or action on his part.

"Come on, let's go into the kitchen and see if your Nana has prepared us anything nice to eat. I'm sure she'll have some treats for you."

David had followed, still feeling upset. Even his favourite rice crispy cakes that his grandmother had been making him since he was really small couldn't cheer him up. He still had a cup of tea to wash down three of them though, even though they didn't make him feel better. He didn't complain when Nana Peters packed up the remainder of them into a Tupperware box and gave them to Jill to take home either. They said goodbye and left, David quiet and withdrawn.

"Did your talk with Granddad help?"

"Not really."

He was glad when his mum went quiet. It suited him fine right now. He didn't want to talk about the subject anymore, he didn't even want to think about it. He decided that spending the afternoon with Billie would be the perfect way to cheer him up after the let down of the morning. He decided he was going to call her the very moment they arrived home.

Chapter Seven

"So, have you seen any more of those…things," Billie asked as they walked towards the public swimming pool, her chosen venue for their afternoon's entertainment.

In spite of the decision he'd made in the early hours of the morning during his mostly sleepless night, David decided not to mention anything else to her right now. It would seem as if it wouldn't affect their friendship after all, so there was no need to rush into it. Besides, he didn't really feel like talking about it at the moment. It wasn't nearly as important or as exciting as he'd thought, so there didn't seem to be anything worth sharing. He shook his head.

"Well, that's good. It is good, isn't it? You don't look like you think it's good, but I think it's good."

"Yes, Billie, it's good."

"Good."

They were silent for a moment then Billie burst into laughter. "Do you realise how many times 'good' was used in what was essentially a non-conversation?"

"I was counting," David replied, grinning back at her. "I'm sure you could have fitted it in a couple of more times if you'd really tried, just for *good* measure."

They dissolved into hysterics, two normal kids having a good time, talking nonsense and laughing together. Everything felt right in David's world again.

They reached the swimming pool, paid, and were given their coloured armbands to wear. Reaching the changing rooms Billie dashed off, giving David a cheery wave and yelling that she would see him soon.

Walking into the boys' changing room, he ignored the wooden bench that ran down the centre and made his way to a cubicle, pulling the curtain firmly closed to undress. Being quite small and skinny for his age, he always felt self-conscious in situations like these. He didn't like his body on display any more than it had to be. The changing room was deserted at the moment but that could change at any minute. Already, he could hear the sounds of splashing, laughter, and the occasional echoing squeal from the pool area itself. It sounded as if it was quite busy, but he supposed that was to be expected during the school holidays. He tried to tell himself that it was okay, that he'd be fine and feel more secure once he was in the water.

Wearing only his trunks and with his arms full of the bundle of clothes and his trainers that he'd gathered up, he made his way over to the allocated locker and stuffed them all in. He hesitated before closing the door, thinking about how Mum would nag him when he went home in his scruffy clothing looking worse than usual because they were all wrinkled. He thought about folding them, then changed his mind. The clock was already ticking on the hour that they'd paid for so why waste time? He slammed the door shut and turned, slipping the rubber band with the key over his wrist.

He gasped as he saw a Hoogle sitting on the wooden bench right in front of him, staggering backwards until he hit the wall of lockers behind him. The thing was disgusting, the green snot dripping from its nose to pool at its feet all over the seat below. It was standing on its hind legs, balancing itself on that kangaroo-like tail. Seeing one up close for the first time while it was standing still and in the bright lights of the changing rooms, he could see that the tail was barbed all the way down to the tip on top – tiny little spikes like thorns on a rose – and he thought he could see little suckers underneath where it curved up to meet the body. It made him think of both a miniature dragon and an octopus at the same time. Its mouth was open, showing those awful teeth, and the hands that were by its side had huge curved talons, as did the ones placed firmly on the bench.

Not dangerous, only mischievous, not dangerous, David chanted in his head, trying to calm his racing heart.

He began to slide along the lockers, making his way slowly and carefully towards the door, still unable to quite believe that something that looked so well equipped to do damage wouldn't harm him. The bottom jaw moved rapidly up and down and it emitted a huffy sort of chattering sound. Its bright green eyes sparkled. It was laughing at him, and it wasn't the first time one had done it!

It was too much for David.

He stuck out his tongue at the creature then turned and bolted, his flash of bravado wearing off just as quickly as it had appeared. He didn't even know where it had come from and wasn't sure if it would chase him or not. He felt petrified. He ran for all he was worth down the empty corridor, splashing his way through the foot bath, then taking a run and leaping into the shallow end of the pool.

"Oi!" a voice shouted. "No running and no diving."

David looked around frantically for the Hoogle, breathing a big sigh of relief when he couldn't see it anywhere. It hadn't chased him down the corridor and into the pool. After seeing that, it didn't seem quite so hard to look up at the angry face of the lifeguard in the red uniform with the whistle around his neck.

"Sorry," he said meekly, hoping he didn't get thrown out.

The last thing he wanted to do was go back to the changing room right now. That thing would likely still be in there, hopping mad at him for his cheekiness. He wondered why it hadn't hunted him down to mess with him in the pool. Maybe they didn't like water, or maybe the chlorine in it would be harmful to them? The thoughts began to calm David but he was careful to keep the apologetic look on his face as the pool attendant regarded him sternly.

Finally, the man seemed to make a decision. "Don't let it happen again," he said, his voice gruff. "I'll be keeping a close eye on you so no more shenanigans."

David breathed a sigh of relief as he watched him stomp off and retake his seat. He knew this particular lifeguard had a reputation for always being grumpy and not liking to see people having too much of a good time. It was the first time David had ever come under his radar and he didn't like the feeling of being singled out for misbehaving. Some gentle ripples in the water beside him alerted him to someone's approach.

"Not like you to do something to upset Crotchety Collins," Billie said in a whisper. "What happened?"

"Hush, if he hears you calling him that, then you'll be in for it!"

"He won't. So what did you do?"

"I was just a little too anxious to get into the water and moving too fast for his liking," David said with a shrug, playing his earlier panic down.

He and Billie might only be friends but he still didn't want to look like a coward in her eyes. He wasn't going to tell her that he was running from a Hoogle. Besides, he wanted to try to forget about the thing and have a good time. He knew he would have to think about it again when their time was up, but he could always try to time his exit so that others were heading to the changing rooms too. For now, he was ready to have some fun. He grinned at Billie, winning her over enough for her to drop the subject. Almost, anyway.

"Well, don't do anything else to catch his attention or we'll get chucked out for sure," she warned. "I'll race you up to the deep end!"

Without waiting for an answer, she dove under the water and began to swim. Laughing, David followed, happy to give her a head start.

Just over half an hour later, they'd raced up and down the length of the pool in all different swimming styles, splashed about, held holding their breath under the water competitions, and were finally starting to tire. Currently, they were in the middle of the pool, holding a 'floating on their backs without letting their legs sink' competition in order to rest a little and get their breath back. David was flapping and flipping his hands back and forth slowly and gently at his sides to keep him in the same place so he didn't float into a swimmer's path, enjoying the feel of the water and marvelling at the resistance that something so soft and fluid could have. He was staring at the rows and rows of bright, square, fluorescent lights along the massive, high ceiling when something odd happened.

The vision above him began to blur.

Thinking he had water in his eyes, he took one hand out of the water and shook it off, closed his eyes tight and then rubbed them. When he opened them again, the ceiling was still blurry. He turned his head, one ear disappearing below the surface and all the sounds around him changing as he heard it from both under and above water in different ears. Normally, he liked the sensation, finding it fascinating to examine how much the body of water could distort things. Today, something else entirely took his attention.

He found he could see everything in his vision – near and far – as clear as day. There was Billie in her black and purple swimsuit, the bold pattern sharp and bright. He could see other people as they passed by, doing the crawl or the breaststroke, the multi-coloured plastic flowers on one woman's swim cap clear and vibrant. He could see the railings that separated the main pool from the shallow pool for the smaller children and babies, could even read the seconds on the large clock mounted on the painted brick wall perfectly. Nothing looked blurry. He turned his head back to stare at the ceiling again.

It was blurry.

In fact, it wasn't just blurry; he could swear that it had started to shimmer. *Was that the right word?* He beetled his brows, confused as to what was going on here. It was a *kind* of shimmering, he decided, but it was also a sort of *wobbling*. He knew that he wasn't making much sense but couldn't think of a better way to describe it to himself, even though he could see it with his own eyes.

"Billie?"

There was no response.

"Billie?" he queried again, louder this time.

Still nothing. He looked at her quickly, seeing she had tipped her head back so that both her ears were underwater. She couldn't hear him. He was about to tap her to attract her attention but hesitated, wanting to take one last look up at the ceiling to ensure that the phenomena was still occurring before he did, just in case it had gone away and he looked like an idiot again. His quick check revealed that it was definitely still happening. She couldn't see the Hoogle, but surely she could see this? He reached out an arm and gently touched her.

Billie raised her head. "Did I win?"

About to speak, David's mouth dropped open and stayed that way as the ceiling above him began to shift. Rendered speechless, he could only point as a large, bright ring appeared around the blurred area. It was pure, brilliant white but it licked and danced wildly like raging flames. David was filled with an icy dread that seemed to chill the very marrow in his bones in spite of the warm water that surrounded him. What was happening?

Suddenly, the ceiling simply wasn't there anymore.

Instead of the polystyrene tiles and square plastic covers over the lights, there was a dense forest, thick stems and giant leaves so impenetrable that David couldn't see beyond them. Instead of brown and green as he would expect, the plants were a mixture of bright blood reds and deep burgundies, giving the whole thing an even more sinister look than any other forest that suddenly appeared in a ceiling would have had.

All of David's senses felt heightened and every one of them was focused on what was on the other side of that hole. His idea that his sight had gone blurry was gone. His vision was now the sharpest it had even been in his life and he knew that what he'd seen had been the reality of it instead of his impression. His hearing too was acute. The sounds of splashing and playing faded away; replaced by the cry of exotic birds and what might be monkey chatters coming down from the ceiling above him. He could feel the sticky, humid heat radiating out from the forest high above.

Instinctively he knew that it was no ordinary forest, that if he could see any of the animals they wouldn't look like the birds or monkeys he would expect to see in a tropical jungle on Earth.

He was looking through a gateway.

He was seeing into another world, into another land.

He had a feeling that even if he hadn't had the chat with his mother and grandfather, he would still know. He didn't know how he possibly could, but he just felt it and knew it was the truth. He'd been born to know.

"David, David!"

"Huh?"

"I've been calling you for ages! I asked what you're pointing at."

Without taking his eyes off the scene above him, David asked Billie the question he was sure he already knew the answer to but had to ask anyway. "You don't see anything unusual up there?"

"Up on the ceiling? No, not even a flickering bulb. What are you...?"

Billie tailed off, suddenly remembering the creature that David had described to her that she couldn't see. "What's up there?" she asked, her voice quiet and fearful.

He knew that there would be no easy answer and this was no time for lengthy tales and explanations. He needed to focus. A gate had opened and he was a Gatekeeper. It was his job to make sure that nothing came through from that other world. A tiny part of him felt proud and important, but mostly, he felt like the terrified thirteen-year-old boy that he was. He didn't have a clue what to do.

Think, David, think! You have to close the gate. But how! I don't know, but there has to be a way! You need to do it quickly!

His own voice screamed at him inside his head. He wished his grandfather had told him more this morning. He wished he was older, wished he was bigger, wished his grandfather or mother was here with him right now, wished for anything at all that would help him. All those thoughts flew from his mind as a massive face suddenly appeared up above, peering down over the edge of the hole. David had no idea what it was, but this was no Hoogle.

The face was at least five times bigger than a Hoogle's, with thick, grey, wrinkled skin and a snout that brought to mind a giant parrot's beak. That snout was twitching up and down as if it was being used to sense and sniff the air around the creature. It had a streak of jet-black feathers that started between its bright yellow, beady eyes and ran up the forehead, over the head, and down to as far as David could see. At first, he thought the thing looked only curious and relatively harmless. It was cocking its head back and forth, like a puppy listening to its owner, and the beaky mouth looked as toothless as an old tortoise. Then it took a really deep sniff.

The beak-like top lip lifted and David saw the single tooth—one long, lethal, rapier-like fang poking down from the roof of its mouth. Those yellow eyes closed and an expression of bliss came over the thing's face as it drank in whatever scent was pleasing it so much. It took a few steps closer to the edge of the hole and revealed its long, snaking neck. Bird-like feet with long, thick claws appeared over the edge, clinging there as it sniffed again, the head swaying back and forth as it savoured the aroma. David was frozen, horrifically fascinated with the thing, unable to move, his mouth still gaping open.

Suddenly, the neck was thrust forward and those beady eyes fixed on him. The thing opened its mouth wide and hissed down at David, a chilling, vicious, threatening sound accompanied by the protrusion and flicking of a black, forked tongue. David barely had time to widen his eyes in horror before the thing launched itself through the gate.

"Billie, swim!" David screamed, scrambling to right himself in the water and shove at his friend.

Billie had been watching David intently, knowing her friend well enough to know that something was going on with him. When he screamed at her, she dove forward and swam, stopping only when she reached the railings that separated the two pools. She turned, expecting David to be right behind her.

He wasn't.

Instead, she saw him almost in the same spot she'd left him, trying to move backwards quickly in the water.

Suddenly, there was an almighty splash right beside him, sending a wave of water washing over him. David screamed.

"David!" Billie cried, immediately letting go of the railings and battling the wash from the splash to get back to him. She might be fighting something invisible but she was going to fight it all the same if she had to.

David was coughing and spluttering; his arms flailing wildly as he tried to escape from the thing that was trying to snag him in its huge claws. He'd seen powerful looking wings folded along its back as it dove from the gateway above, had seen another set of three talons protruding from them also. He had no doubt that it could pick him up and fly away with him, stealing him through the gate into another world. He didn't know what it would do with him after that, but he had a strong feeling that the scent it had been enjoying as much as he enjoyed the scent of sizzling bacon had been him, and the other people in the pool.

He had to figure out how to deal with this. This was his responsibility now. That thought was even more terrifying than the creature, but if it was even half as vicious as it looked, then the lives of everyone here could be in his hands.

"It's all in the mind, boy."

David heard the voice behind him but was too busy trying to duck and dive as the long, snaky neck bobbed and weaved following his every move. He ignored the deep baritone, knowing he must look crazy to any onlooker.

"To send it back. It's all in the head."

That got David's attention. The man wasn't referring to his dubious mental state and assuming he was fighting an imaginary enemy after all. He seemed to know something about the gates. "Can you help?"

"Not anymore, not since three weeks ago. Just focus."

Focus on what? David wanted to scream, but he knew he didn't know the rules. Maybe the man wasn't allowed to tell him, maybe he was supposed to learn his lessons on his own and the man had told him too much already. Not really knowing what he was doing, he focused on the only thing he could think of—imagining the monster being yanked up out of the water by an invisible force and pulled back towards the hole. He imagined it as hard as he possibly could through his fears, trying to push them aside to concentrate fully on the imagery.

Nothing happened.

I must be doing it wrong, he thought, about to give up and give in to his panic when he noticed that the monster wasn't trying to get him anymore. It seemed instead to be fighting something else entirely, something that David couldn't see.

"Keep going," the voice said.

Surprised, David did.

To his amazement, the thing began to rise out of the water. Thrashing and flailing but seemingly helpless against whatever was dragging it up into the air, it screeched a terrible, high-pitched screech of rage and frustration. David whooped and focused even harder, his small amount of success giving him confidence and strength. He imagined the thing flying up through the air, propelled, then tossed a long, long way into the gateway above, far away from the entrance to this world.

The next thing he knew, it was actually happening. The thing was flying up through the air bullet fast, just as he'd pictured it, and then it shot through the gate and disappeared. "Yes," he screamed, punching the air. "I did it!"

"Keep your voice down and close the gate."

David finally turned to see an unassuming old man. Except for small tufts of grey hair above each ear, his head was bald. His skin was wrinkly, his chest sunken. He would never have placed the deep, calm, commanding voice with the figure he saw before him. He stared in amazement.

"Stop gawping and get on with it, before something else comes through," the old man said.

David found his own voice, which he thought sounded small and pathetic in comparison. "How?"

The withering stare he received in return told him all he needed to know. "Oh, I think I get it. The same way?"

The man shook his head, muttering about young 'uns these days and something about ignorance. David turned his attention to the hole in the ceiling and did a similar thing as he'd done before, imaging it slamming shut and the ceiling returning to normal. It seemed to take every bit of strength he had but finally, it happened. After what felt like forever, but was probably only a minute or so, nothing was above him except those bland tiles and bright lights. He collapsed back in the water, completely exhausted.

"Are you all right?" Billie asked, having reached him, but not being able to find a single thing to do to help.

"I'm fine," David managed to gasp. "Just weak."

"Harrumph."

David remembered the man that had helped and realised he needed to thank him, even if he was a touch on the derisive side and seemed a little scornful of David's success. "Thank you for your assistance, sir. I wouldn't have been able to do it without you."

"I'll say," the man responded before he began to turn away.

"Wait, sir!"

The man ignored him and continued to move away. David wondered if he should go after him thinking he should at least know his name, but a loud, repetitive sound was taking his attention. It dawned on him that it was a whistle.

"Uh oh, Crotchety Collins is looking right at us," Billie said. "And he seems to be signalling for us to come over."

"I suppose we'd better go," David said.

Wearily, David swam back to the shallow end of the pool to where the attendant was waiting, red faced and furious. "How dare you ignore me calling you for so long? I don't know what you were doing to cause all that splashing and ruckus, but I warned you already to behave. Out, the pair of you!"

David didn't even bother to argue or try to defend himself. With having to keep what had really happened a secret, there was nothing he could say anyway. As tired as he was, Billie had to give him a push to get him up the last few of the metal steps out of the pool. They splashed their way back through the foot bath together and stopped when they came to the point where they would have to part.

"I'll meet you at the coffee bar," Billie said. "You've got a lot of talking to do. Something major was happening back there, I could see it in the way you were acting. I want to know exactly what's going on, David, and I don't want any of your evasiveness. I overheard some of what that guy said anyway. You owe me a massive explanation."

"Fair enough," David said, resigned. He'd intended to do it at some point anyway. This only meant it would happen earlier than expected. "I'll see you soon."

Once he'd showered, dressed, and was towel drying his hair quickly while seated on the moulded plastic seat in the cubicle, David started to tremble all over. He knew that it was the onset of shock; he'd read about it and seen it on television. He really should get to the coffee bar and have something with sugar in it, but he was so tired that the thought of moving seemed impossible. He leant back against the plastic wall. If only he could close his eyes just for a second…

He might have fallen asleep for goodness knows how long if a wheezy, huffy chortle hadn't jolted him awake. He looked up at the curtain rail where the sound had come from. A Hoogle was sitting up there, pointing and huffing away at him.

"Don't even think about it," David said, "or you'll be next. I'll throw you so hard through a gate you'll end up in the middle of next week in the other world."

The Hoogle made a squawking sound, and then it was gone. David sighed. He really ought to force himself to move. Billie would be waiting for him and she'd be worried if he took too long. He rose to his feet, weaving about slightly unsteadily until he found his balance.

Concentrating on putting one foot in front of the other, he wearily made his way out of the changing rooms to go and join his friend.

Chapter Eight

David was almost surprised to find himself waking up to see that night had fallen and darkness had settled in around him.

He glanced at the digital readout on his clock radio, stunned that it was after 9 pm. When had he come up to his room and lay down? When had he fallen asleep? It took a moment, his brain struggling to sort out reality from the dream he'd been having and to put all the pieces from the time before he'd dozed off together. Then he remembered. He turned on his lamp before sitting up and leaning against his headboard, running a hand over his face as everything that had happened that afternoon came flooding back. He allowed himself to go over it step by step in order to make more sense of it and to bring him out of that feeling that he hated, the one where he wasn't quite sure if he was awake or not, or what was real and what wasn't.

He'd arrived in the coffee bar to find that Billie had beaten him there and had already queued in line, chosen and paid for their snacks, and taken their tray to a table. He'd sat down and gratefully accepted the large glass of orange juice that she pushed towards him, along with the packet of crisps and the chocolate brownie. She'd waited patiently until he'd devoured them all before she spoke.

"Feeling better?"

"A little," he replied, feeling the trembling begin to lessen and a tiny scrap of strength return as the sugar and vitamin C entered his system.

Once he'd felt up to it, Billie made him talk. He'd told her everything he could, from his experience with what felt like hundreds of Hoogles at his birthday dinner, the talks with his mother and grandfather, and finally describing everything that he'd seen in the pool. Just as a good friend should, Billie had listened to it all without interruption. However, once he'd stopped, she was free to ask questions.

"So who was that man standing beside you?"

"I have no idea. I wanted to ask his name so I could maybe thank him properly when I wasn't in shock, but he left before I could."

"He must have been another Gatekeeper," Billie declared.

David looked at her with pride. He'd just told her the most outlandish story and she hadn't scoffed, hadn't doubted, and hadn't even laughed at him. She'd simply taken it all as the truth because he was the one telling her, because she wanted to believe him and therefore she would because they were best friends. She didn't even look frightened to learn about all the other worlds and the unknown creatures that lurked there. She'd paled a little when she'd heard the description of what had been so close to her in the swimming pool, but David thought she'd taken it all very well.

"I suppose he must have been, although he said he couldn't help. I don't know. I'm too tired to think it all through and put it all together right now. I feel so weak," David said.

"I'm going to go and call Jill. You're not fit to walk home."

"I'm fine, honestly."

"No, you're not. You might feel not so bad sitting here, but I bet you'll feel wiped out again after only a few steps. She won't mind, especially once all this has been explained to her."

"Okay then, yes, I would be really grateful for a lift home. Billie, before you go, there's something else I need to say."

"Go on."

"Mum warned me not to mention this to anyone. She was so emphatic about it that I didn't have the guts to tell her that I'd already told you about the Hoogle. As far as she's aware, you don't know anything, and it seems to be a pretty big rule. I don't know what would happen if anyone found out that I'd broken the rules already. I might be stripped of the title, or the ability, or whatever."

"Looking at you now, that might be a good thing. I'm not sure you are cut out for this," Billie said, chewing her bottom lip. "No offence."

"None taken, I'm not sure either. I know I'm no athlete and not exactly the great warrior type. I'm not even very brave."

"Oh, I wouldn't say that," she'd said, giving him an encouraging smile. "After all, just think of what you confronted in there. You might have been scared but you still faced up to your responsibilities."

David had blushed, beaming with pride. "I suppose so," he'd conceded, not knowing if his actions were brave or not but proud to have Billie think so highly of him regardless.

"I'll go and make that call. Here, finish my juice, I've had enough and you need it more than I do."

David had sipped on the juice, holding the glass in both hands just to be safe. When Billie returned, she'd made a face. "It wasn't your mum that answered the phone, it was Candy. She said Jill was busy in the garden. Sorry, but she wheedled out of me why I was calling and immediately said there was no need to bother Jill, that she'd come and pick us up."

"Great, that's all we need."

It hadn't been as bad as he'd expected. Billie had taken the front seat next to Candy and kept her occupied by asking her questions about hair products or some other girly thing. David, having crawled into the back seat, had closed his eyes and let the conversation wash over him. When they'd pulled up outside Billie's house, she offered him a sympathetic smile.

"Sorry," she'd mouthed, and David knew she was referring to leaving him alone with Candy. "I promise I'll call you first thing tomorrow."

She'd given him a final wave before she ran up her path and into the house.

"Do you want to move into the front with me," Candy had asked.

"I'm fine here, thanks."

Although David had seen Candy glance at him several times in the rear view mirror, even she'd seemed to realise he wasn't up to talking and for once had been unusually quiet on the last leg of their journey home. She'd stuck close to him after parking in the driveway, remaining a step behind him all the way as they walked into the house. He'd wondered exactly how bad he'd looked for her to think that was necessary. It seemed as if Candy was expecting him to collapse any minute and for her to have to catch him when he did.

Once inside, he'd declared he wasn't feeling well and headed up to his room. Candy must have immediately reported to Jill because David had only just changed into his pyjamas and was crawling into bed when he heard a knock on his door. His mum poked her head around after he'd called for whomever it was to come in. He'd just managed to tell her the story before he couldn't keep his eyes open a moment longer and snuggled down just in time before falling into a deep sleep.

Now it was more than five hours later. He couldn't believe he'd slept so long. Not only that, but he still felt tired. He considered getting up, dressed, and going downstairs. He was sure that his Mum would have kept some dinner aside for him. He really couldn't be bothered even though he was hungry. He just didn't have the energy. Instead, he stepped out of his room to go to the bathroom, wash his face, brush his teeth, and go to bed properly. He was startled when he almost ran into Candy out on the landing.

"Oh, hi."

"Hi there," she said brightly, not seeming to be the least bit bothered that she'd been caught apparently loitering outside his bedroom door. "Feeling better?"

"A bit, thanks."

"Good. Jill said you could have a tray in your room if you woke up. Shall I get it for you? Dinner was macaroni cheese," she added in a singsong voice as if doing her best to tempt him.

He was about to refuse when his tummy gave a very loud rumble. Candy laughed. "Okay, I'm taking that as a yes. Tuck yourself back into bed and I'll be up with it in just a minute."

True to her word, Candy arrived with a tray laid out with a loaded plateful, a glass, and a chilled can of fizzy pop. "Here, let me put this down quick before I break a nail," she said, positioning it on his lap and checking if it was steady before letting go. "Tuck in."

It looked as if she was going to stand over him and watch him eat. He carefully reached for the book on his bedside cabinet, giving Candy a pointed look as he picked it up.

"Oh sure, right, leave you in peace, I get it. Jill said if you eat all that, there's Swiss roll and custard for dessert if you want. I'll come back and check in a bit to see."

She gave him a little wave and a wink before leaving the room, closing the door firmly behind her. David breathed a sigh of relief. He pulled open the tab of his pop and poured some into the glass before setting the can on the bedside cabinet, too intent on his task and trying not to spill to notice that he didn't hear Candy's heels walking away from his bedroom door down the landing.

***

Downstairs, Jill was cleaning the already gleaming kitchen for the third time, a worried frown marring her usually cool and composed features.

"If you do that once more, you're going to scrub all the varnish off those doors and wear right through the granite," William said.

Jill looked up and sighed as she gave William a resigned smile. She toyed with the cloth still in her hand. "I know, but you know I clean when I'm on edge."

"Still worried about David?"

While David had slept earlier, Jill had managed to corner William and quickly recount what he'd told her about the happenings at the swimming pool that afternoon. They hadn't had much time before Andrew had come looking for her, but she'd got most of it out before they'd been interrupted.

"Yes, I am."

"Does he know that you're worried?"

"Oh heavens, no! At least I hope not. I think I did a pretty good job keeping it to myself. I just smiled a lot and told him that he'd done a terrific job and that he was going to make a wonderful Gatekeeper. He seemed rather traumatised by the whole experience, so there was no way I was going to make it worse."

"I'm not quite sure what the problem is then. He might have been shaken up by it, but he handled it and no one was hurt. He did what he was supposed to do and no doubt he'll do it again and do even better next time. Is this just the whole protective mother thing?"

"Well, partly I suppose. No mother can ever really be that happy that her child is a Gatekeeper, no matter how proud we are. It's dangerous and it's a constant worry every time they leave the house, but it's more than just that. I can't help thinking that everything is happening too fast. It's too much, too soon. We know that the duty transfers on the day of the thirteen birthday – it's the same for every Gatekeeper – but somehow it usually works out that they have a little time to come to terms with it and learn before they have anything more than the Hoogle to deal with, let alone an actual gate."

"Maybe we just live in a hot spot for gates."

Jill shook her head. "Everywhere is pretty much a hot spot for gates. It's the gates that open that we have to worry about and as far as I've always been aware, that doesn't happen around here that often."

"Then it was simply overdue. Either that or we've had exceptional Gatekeepers who've done their job so well over the years that even someone who knows all about it hasn't noticed the gates opening."

Jill looked doubtful but she was hopeful that it could provide at least part of the explanation. "Maybe. I still can't help but add it to the other things, though. Don't forget that he did see a Hoogle a day early, and then on his actual birthday he saw masses of them, not just the normal one or two. I've never heard of that happening before, especially the day early part."

"Did you speak to your dad about it?"

"Not yet. There hasn't really been the opportunity. I didn't want to mention it in front of David. I want him to think that this is as normal as possible. It's always such a shock to begin with, so I didn't want to add to that."

"Maybe you should give Geoff a call?"

Jill glanced at the clock on the cooker. "It's a bit late to ring him tonight. I'll give him a call in the morning. I'm hoping he'll tell me lots of stories of this sort of thing happening to others. I really don't want to think of David as being special or singled out in any way; well, not any more than being a Gatekeeper makes him special, or singles him out as it is, I mean," she finished with a laugh.

"I knew what you meant," William replied, walking over and wrapping his arms around her in a comforting hug. "I'm sure everything's going to be just fine."

"I hope so, William. I really hope so."

***

Back upstairs, Candy listened carefully at David's door. There was absolute silence. No sounds of any movement, no sound of a fork clinking against china, nothing. She went to the top of the stairs and cocked her head. She could hear Andrew laughing at something on the television he was watching in the den, could hear the low murmur of voices as Jill and William talked in the kitchen. Everyone was occupied with doing their own thing, secure in the knowledge that David was safely tucked up in bed, and no one was thinking about her or what she might be doing. They probably assumed she was curling her hair, painting her nails, or doing some of her other beauty regimes. That suited her just fine. Without knocking, she gently and slowly opened David's door a crack, peeking in.

Still sitting up, the tray still on his lap, he'd fallen fast asleep. The hand that had been holding his book had fallen by his side and the book lay beside it, closed without the bookmark in so that his place had been lost. His mouth was slightly open and his chest was moving up and down with his slow, deep breathing. Glancing at the tray, Candy saw he'd only eaten about half of the food on his plate before he'd succumbed and fallen into a deep sleep. She picked up the tray and carried it out onto the landing, laying it on the floor before going back into the room.

She paused as David murmured when she picked up the book, waiting until he settled before placing it on the bedside cabinet. He stirred again when she did. She stood silently, holding her breath, waiting to see if he was going to wake up and find her standing over him. He didn't. He murmured some more then snuggled down onto his pillows, pulled the duvet up to his shoulders, and went straight back to sleep without opening his eyes. Candy smiled down at him, thinking how small and vulnerable he looked.

Chapter Nine

When David woke the next morning, he couldn't believe how late he'd slept. It was already way past ten and the weak October sunshine was brightening his room through his curtains. He felt groggy and confused. The last thing he remembered was reading his book and eating his dinner in bed. With a shrug, he decided that his mum must have come in, taken everything away, and tucked him in, not wanting to wake him after his eventful day—a bit *too* eventful if he was honest. This whole Gatekeeper thing was going to be a whole lot scarier than he'd thought.

Yes, the Hoogle had terrified him at first, but once he'd heard about them being mischievous and harmless, he'd thought this whole thing sounded as if it might be fun. Granddad had made it sound like no big deal and nothing special. He'd been on the verge of believing and accepting that. He could see now that he'd been very wrong on both counts. This wasn't some great, make-believe adventure or some fantasy game. This was very real, and he was beginning to see that it was going to be very dangerous. He definitely wasn't ready for all this. Still, he didn't seem to have much choice in the matter. He couldn't spend the rest of his life lying in bed and hiding from it all, no matter how tempting the idea was.

Fifteen minutes later, he padded downstairs barefoot, his hair still wet from his shower. As always, Jill was in the kitchen awaiting his arrival. The radio was on and she was humming along to the tune, her hips swaying in time to the beat as she stood leaning on the countertop. She smiled at him, the gesture as full of warmth and sunshine as the brightly coloured outfit she wore. David thought she was like one of the exotic birds he would often see on the nature programmes he loved so much. The sight of her and the familiarity of it all immediately made him feel better.

"Morning, Mum."

"Morning, love, how are you feeling?"

"I'm fine," he said in response, not even knowing where to begin to explain the turmoil that was bubbling inside of him.

"Hungry?"

He nodded and Jill's smile widened, glad to see that yesterday's events hadn't made him lose his appetite. She did want to talk to him about yesterday, but first thing in the morning wasn't the time and she didn't want to push him. He would say more if she left him to talk about things when he was ready and not before. "Well, I suppose you're a teenage boy now, you're likely always hungry. What would you like for breakfast? I reckon you deserve something special."

"Just cereal and toast will be fine, thank you. Is there any message from Billie?"

Jill frowned and shook her head. "No, were you expecting one?"

David shrugged. "She said she'd call first thing so I assumed I'd missed her since I'd slept so late."

"She's likely having a long lie-in herself; it is the holidays after all. You can give her a call after breakfast and see if she's up yet."

David nodded in agreement while already diving into his bowl of cereal eagerly with his spoon. He didn't know if it was anything to do with being a teenager now or not, but his stomach was certainly protesting the fact that he'd only eaten half his dinner last night before falling asleep and had missed out on dessert.

When he'd finished, he rinsed his dishes under the sink and loaded them into the dishwasher. "Okay, can I go and call Billie?"

"Of course, dear."

Five minutes later, David was back in the kitchen, a worried and puzzled look on his face. "Mum, what were you doing this morning? You weren't vacuuming or anything, anything that might mean you missed the phone or doorbell?"

"Definitely not. I've been in the kitchen nearly all morning. Everyone wants breakfast at different times before heading out. I certainly would have heard either of them. What's the problem?"

David scratched his head. "Well, Billie's mum said she was up practically at the break of dawn and down in the kitchen preparing enough food for a small army. She packed it into her backpack and headed out before 7 am. She was certain she was going to call me so we could go for one of her epic hikes. She's a bit worried that I haven't heard from her, and so am I."

Jill gave it some thought before she spoke. "You know, you and Billie have been inseparable since you were very small, but just as you're growing up, so is she. You have to remember that, and maybe consider that she might just want a day on her own to think about things she might be going through right now, or even that she might want to do more…well…girly things."

David shook his head emphatically. "If this was someone else, I might have bought that, but not Billie. She's never going to be a girly girl, and I know if she packed a ton of food and took her backpack then she was definitely going for a hike. Besides, she promised she would call me and she would never break a promise, I'm sure of it."

"It would be unlike her, I agree, but people are allowed to change their minds you know. Why don't you go and get some socks and shoes on and grab your jacket? I can drive you around for a bit and see if we can spot her, if that will put your mind at rest. Maybe she was on her way over and ran into someone. Maybe they're still standing, chatting, or maybe she changed her plans and went into town with them or something instead. I bet she's sitting in the food court right now, drinking a milkshake and eating a hamburger, forgetting all about the sandwiches she made in her backpack."

David brightened. "Now that does sound like Billie! Skipping the call to just turn up but getting side-tracked on the way would be just like her. Thanks for the offer of driving around to check out some of the places she might be, but I think I'll give her another hour. I'm sure that's what happened so she'll turn up here eventually."

"Let me know if you change your mind," Jill said.

He nodded and smiled, relieved now he felt he had an explanation. He had enough on his plate at the moment without his best friend doing a disappearing act.

Up in his room, sprawled on his bed with a book open in front of him, his bare feet waving in the air behind him, David was reading half-heartedly. Most of his thoughts were on yesterday and the creature he'd seen, and the rest of them were on Billie. His eyes kept drifting towards the clock on his bedside cabinet, watching the minutes pass by. He felt tense; his muscles partially poised to leap into action and race downstairs should the doorbell or phone ring.

Downstairs, going about her chores for the day, Jill was also thinking about Billie. Although she hadn't been overly concerned at first, the more that she thought about it, the more it did seem a little strange. It wasn't like Billie to let David down, even if she could be a little scatterbrained at times. For the first time since hearing about the incident at the pool yesterday, Jill wondered what Billie had made of what she'd seen. She wouldn't have seen much since she wasn't a Gatekeeper. She couldn't possibly be one of those since she had an older brother at University and Gatekeepers were always only children. Jill didn't know why that was the case, but knew it was one of the rules. However, even though Billie wouldn't have seen the gate or the creature, she must have noticed something odd was happening with David, and being the type of good friend she was, she'd likely questioned him until she'd received a satisfactory answer. With a sense of horror, it finally dawned on Jill that David might have told Billie everything. If he had, she could be in great danger. Maybe her unexpected silence today wasn't as innocent as she'd first thought. She needed to find out for certain.

Abandoning the basket of laundry she'd been sorting into piles, she dashed upstairs and knocked on David's door.

"Come in," David called.

She opened the door and walked in, pulling up his desk chair in front of the bed to sit facing him.

David looked surprised. She always sat on the edge of the bed beside him. He swallowed. He had a feeling whatever she was about to say was very serious. He wondered if he was in trouble for something. He was wracking his brains as to what he might have done when Jill cleared her throat and began.

"David, I'm about to ask you a very important question and I want you to tell me the truth, no matter how much trouble you think it might get you into, okay?"

David swallowed again and licked his lips, but he nodded his agreement.

"Did you tell Billie about the gate and the creature yesterday?"

The way his face flushed and he averted his eyes from hers would have told Jill everything she needed to know even if he hadn't answered. "Yes." It was no more than a whisper, but it was loud enough for Jill to catch.

"How much did you tell her about it?"

"Everything," he muttered. "I told her everything."

"That's what I was afraid of," Jill said with a sigh.

With his cheeks still aflame, David tried to stammer his way through an explanation. "I had to, Mum. You see, I'd already told her about the Hoogle I'd seen before you'd explained anything to me, when I didn't know that I wasn't supposed to say anything to anyone. I was scared and I didn't know where else to turn, or who else might believe me. Grownups never believe this sort of thing in books so I just thought that Billie of all people would be the one to listen and take me seriously."

"Did she?"

"I don't think she did at first, but she thought about it overnight and came to the conclusion that I wouldn't lie to her. She definitely believed that *I* believed I'd seen it, and that was enough for her to believe. She told me so. Then, when you told me about this great responsibility I would have, I was worried that keeping a secret as big as that would damage our friendship. I wanted to tell her straight away but I didn't. But when the whole thing happened at the pool, she didn't know what was going on, but she put it together that it was connected to the creature I'd seen. I had to tell her. There didn't seem to be anything else I could do. I'm sorry, Mum, I really am."

"It's okay. I do understand, although it would have been better if it hadn't happened."

"We can trust Billie. She won't tell another living soul because I asked her not to."

"I don't doubt it and that's not what's concerning me at the moment. I'll have to think about that part later, but for now, it doesn't matter."

David, from being flushed, suddenly turned deathly pale. "You don't think her not turning up today had anything to do with me telling her, do you? It couldn't be! I only told her yesterday and you're the only person that knows I told her. She couldn't possibly be in danger already. She couldn't, could she, Mum?"

"I hope not, David," Jill replied, reaching over to give his hair a stroke. "It would seem a bit unlikely that someone would have found out and come after her this quickly. Why don't I give her mother another call and see if she's turned up back home and if she hasn't, we could take that drive."

David was downstairs in minutes with his socks and shoes on, hopping from foot to foot while he waited impatiently for his mother to hang up the phone. He couldn't determine what was happening from her end of the conversation alone as she was only saying yes and making a lot of agreeable sympathetic noises. It seemed to take forever but she finally replaced the handset in its base and turned to David.

"Mrs. Thomson was just about to call here and ask if she'd appeared yet. She was certain she was on her way to see you."

"So she's not home then," David said, a statement more than a question.

"No, not yet, but I'm certain that if anyone can find her it'll be you. You know all her favourite places to go. Come on; let's head out so at least we're doing something."

They climbed into the car and drove off. David directed his mother, first looking around their own neighbourhood, checking out the places he and Billie liked to hang out. Coming up empty, they headed into town, driving around all the places he knew Billie likes to go. His mum would drop him off where necessary and he would jump out of the car and run inside to look. He peered down from the gallery at the swimming pool, seeing if he could spot her familiar form in the water. He checked at the ice rink. He looked in all her favourite stores at the shopping centre, feeling self-conscious and awkward as he walked through the aisles of girls' clothing and accessories, jewellery and makeup. He checked the food court seating area and the queues at her favourite food counters. He checked the bookstore and the music shop. He even checked the library, although he knew it was unlikely she would ever go there without him dragging her there. They drove around the town square several times, looking to see if she'd ran into others from school and was simply hanging out there like many of them did, some messing around on skateboards or rollerblades, others just loitering for the sake of it, trying to look cool. She was nowhere to be found.

"I'm out of ideas for the town," David said to Jill, feeling utterly defeated. "And we've checked the route from her house to mine a million times. I can only think of one other place she would be, and that's hiking in the woods."

"You really think she would have gone to do that without you?"

"I didn't think so before, but after what you said this morning it might be possible, maybe with…ummm…well, you know…puberty and all." He blushed as he said it, staring out of the car window, unable to look Jill in the eye as he mentioned the subject. It seemed as if today was doomed to be filled with awkward and uncomfortable topics. "Take me home and I'll pack my backpack and go looking for her there, although if she did go for some privacy, she might not thank me."

"I'm sure she'd understand when she realises everyone is worried about her, but I'm not so sure I can let you do that. It's a bit late in the day. You won't get far before you'd have to turn back or be caught out there in the dark."

"I can make it to the treehouse and back, I know I can. Please, Mum? It's our best shot and the most likely place. If I hadn't been hung up on the idea that she wouldn't have gone alone, then I'd have tried there first of all. I have to know if she's there. I have to find her. I'll be super quick, I promise."

Jill glanced at the clock on the dashboard, chewing her lip. She didn't want to deny him when she could see how anxious he was, but the thought of him being out in the woods alone in the dark terrified her. "Maybe I could come with you?"

He shook his head. "You'd only slow me down and then we'd definitely be caught out after dark. No offence, of course, but you're not used to it like we are. I can move quickly. I'd be worried you'd trip or fall so I'd have to go slower if you came."

"Yes, all right," Jill said speeding up a little, heading home in a determined manner now that she'd made the decision. "But I'm dropping you off at the edge of the path you usually take and I'm going to be waiting for you there before dusk. You'd better be back by then young man or I'm coming in there to get you and you won't like it when I find you."

"I will be, I promise."

Chapter Ten

David kept his gaze facing forward, determined not to give in to his urge to look around him and glance back over his shoulder nervously. In one hand, he held a small torch and in the other, he clutched the compass Billie had given him for his birthday, more as a talisman than to guide his way. He'd misjudged the timing, the journey to the treehouse always seeming much quicker because he'd always had Billie with him to pass the time. Now it was dusk and the woods were getting absolutely creepy.

Come on, you're not a little kid anymore, he told himself, focusing on putting one foot in front of the other. *Besides, you must be nearly back.* He had to admit that with the fading light he wasn't so sure of his direction or exactly where he was anymore, even though he'd walked this route a thousand times and would have sworn he could have done it blindfold. He would never make that claim again. He was beginning to wish he'd listened to his mum and not attempted this in the time he had left of the shorter hours of October daylight. He kept on putting one foot in front of the other, fighting off the almost overwhelming instinct to run. If he did, he would definitely get lost, or risk falling and injuring himself. The worst of it all was that he hadn't found Billie. In fact, he hadn't found any sign of her at all.

He'd examined their normal pathway to the treehouse in great detail, using everything he'd learned about tracking from television programmes and books to see if he could spot tracks or signs that someone had walked that way recently. He'd hunted meticulously for any clues or indications of recent activity around and inside the treehouse itself. He'd come up empty on everything. It looked like he'd been wrong in all his guesses. He was utterly devastated. He was certain that he'll be the one to find her because he thought he knew her best. As lost in his own bleak thoughts as he was, it took him a moment to register the sounds that were coming from behind him. A chill of fear crawled over his skin as he finally realised it sounded as if there were a second set of footsteps stepping in time with his own. He halted, listening to see if he could determine what the sounds were, but when he stopped, they stopped.

Telling himself it was merely the sound of his own footsteps echoing in the near silent woods, he carried on. The sounds started up again. He stopped. They stopped. It had to be the night playing tricks on him. He started up again, this time altering his pace, speeding up, slowing down, all the while trying to make it look as if it were the terrain that was causing him to do so. He'd just speeded up once more when this time he came to a sudden halt mid step, one foot in the air.

Aha! Another footstep, paw step, hoof step, or whatever, crunched behind him. He'd caught it out! With a gulp, he realised that wasn't a good thing, not a good thing at all. Someone, or *something,* was following him.

It had stopped now, presumably waiting to see what his next move would be, waiting to see if he knew. He tried to tell himself it was simply a curious woodland animal, maybe a deer used to being fed by hikers, loitering around to see if there were any spoils to be had tonight, or maybe a badger ensuring that he didn't get too close to its sett. He tried desperately to make his brain see those things. Instead, it envisioned the Hoogle, and monstrous, dinosaur birds, and all other manner of weird and nightmarish creatures that didn't belong in his world. The instinct to run was screaming inside him now. He didn't. He fought it…hard.

David decided that trying to play it clever was his best bet. After all, he had a rough idea of the mental capacity of most normal animals, but had no idea of the intelligence of these other worldly creatures that snuck or exploded through open gates. He pretended to listen hard then laughed aloud and shook his head at himself, as if he were being a complete idiot for giving in to paranoia. After that, he walked on at a steady pace, whistling as he went, trying to keep the tremble from tune. His only thought was that if whatever was following him knew it had been detected, then it would have no more need for stealth. No need for stealth and secrecy could mean an all-out attack. If he was lucky, his ruse would work and the unknown entity would continue to await the perfect opportunity until it was too late. He just *had* to be nearly back to the road by now. He tried to keep his pounding heart in check as he walked on.

Suddenly, a figure stepped out from the trees, looming large in front of him. Just as he let out a gasp, he thought he heard a catlike hiss behind him. The panic that he'd been holding at bay threatened to overtake him once and for all. Was he surrounded? A scream formed in his throat but before he had a chance to release it, a torch clicked on and was shone in his face, blinding him. He flung up a hand to shield his eyes from the brilliant onslaught of light.

"David? David, is that you?"

"Andrew!" David cried, hearing the childlike relief and desperation in his own voice.

He was too relieved to be embarrassed about it. Still trying to shield his eyes, he rushed forward, flinging himself at Andrew. His stepfather caught him and wrapped his arms around him. David had to choke back sobs as Andrew let his own relief be heard in his voice.

"Thank heavens I've found you safe and sound. I've been so worried. Oh, thank goodness you're all right. I don't know what I would have done if I hadn't found you."

"Me neither," David admitted, his face still pressed hard against Andrew's slightly out of shape bulk. "I'm sorry I thought I would have been back before it got dark."

"It's okay, you're safe now, and that's all that matters. Come on; let's get back to the car quickly. Your mum and dad are beside themselves, as you can imagine. Your dad is at home, just in case there is any news. Mum is here and wanted to be out looking for you too, but I asked her to wait in the car in case you appeared. The last thing I needed was two people I love lost in the woods at night."

"I'm sorry I caused so much trouble. I just really thought I'd find Billie."

Andrew placed a hand on his shoulder and kept it there as they walked. "No luck then?"

"No," David said, shaking his head sadly. "Has anyone heard from her?"

"I hate to be the bearer of bad news but no, she hasn't turned up yet. I'm sorry. Looking for you and not being able to find you for the last hour or so has given me a taste of how you and her family must be feeling, so I do understand how frantic you must be. If there's anything I can do all you have to do is ask. You know I'm always here for you, even if it's only to listen."

"Thanks, Andrew. I really appreciate that. You've really been out here for an hour?"

"I'd have been out for longer than that if I'd known what was going on sooner. Jill only called me at work when she arrived at the start of the path and you weren't there. She told me she was about to head into the woods to try to find you. I made her promise to stay put and dashed straight over here. I'd have stayed out all night if that's what it took. I would never give up on you."

David was immensely gratified to hear how much Andrew cared about him. It made him feel safe and secure. It also made him feel worse about Billie. "Am I giving up on Billie if I go home now?"

"No, definitely not. Her parents have called everyone they know to form search parties. They've called the police, and since she's a minor that didn't turn up where she was expected to be several hours ago, they're finally paying attention. They're doing everything they can. I know you're growing up and aren't a kid anymore, but you're still a minor too. If we hadn't found you we would've had to report you missing too, using up valuable resources looking for both of you instead of concentrating on her. You're actually doing the best thing for Billie by being home safe."

"I hadn't thought of it that way," David replied, still sounding a little doubtful but understanding the logic.

"I'll tell you what. I'll take the day off tomorrow and you and I will form our own little search party if you like."

"That would be great, thank you."

They walked the rest of the way in silence, David realising that his estimation hadn't been far off; he was almost back after all. Jill was waiting there by the two cars, pacing up and down. She burst into tears as she saw them emerge together from the treeline and then confused herself trying to hug them both at the same time, not knowing whether to thank Andrew or greet David and tell him how happy she was to see him. If she'd been beside herself with worry before, she was practically high as a kite with relief now. Any other time, if he hadn't been so worried about Billie, David might have laughed and teased her, but he couldn't quite find it in himself to find anything funny right now.

Once everyone had their fill of hugs, they decided that David would go home with Jill. She was too reluctant to let him out of sight to allow him to go with Andrew. The adults got into the driving seats of their respective cars and David climbed into the passenger side beside his mum. Just as he was about to pull the door shut, he thought he heard something dashing through the forest at high speed, crashing through the undergrowth, twigs snapping, fallen leaves crunching. It seemed to confirm what David had suspected—Andrew hadn't been the only one hunting him in the woods that night. Whatever it was wasn't trying to stay quiet any longer. It had no need. The sounds it was making were getting quieter. It was running away from them, not at them.

"Ready?" Jill asked, a less than subtle hint for David to shut the door.

He gave his mother a fake smile and nodded, pulling the door closed and fastening his seatbelt. He had absolutely no idea what to make of what he'd just heard, or any of it for that matter. His days only seemed to be getting stranger and more frightening. He dreaded to imagine what might come next.

Chapter Eleven

David spent yet another restless night, tossing and turning, unable to enjoy being warm and cosy in his bed as he thought about Billie being out there somewhere unknown. Was she lost? Was she cold? Worst of all, was she frightened? He tried to take comfort in the fact that there were lots of people looking for her, responsible adults, people he could trust: her family, their friends, neighbours, the police. They would all be doing their utmost to bring her home to safety. The thought didn't help much, especially now that he knew that on top of all the terrible and dreadful things in this world, there was added danger that the majority of people knew nothing about. His imagination was running wild with thoughts of all the things that could have happened to her. In the end, he'd given up trying to sleep and had turned on his light, spending the night just sitting up in bed, worrying and fretting and hoping to hear the ringing of the house phone. He knew Mrs. Thomson, Billie's mum, would call the minute she was found, no matter what the hour.

The call hadn't come.

David felt utterly dejected as he headed downstairs the next morning. He brightened a little at the sight of Andrew in the kitchen with his mum, still home and dressed in more casual clothing than the smart trousers and shirt he usually wore on weekdays. He wasn't going in to work, he was staying at home, to help look for Billie, just as he'd promised. David didn't expect Andrew to let him down as such, but had wondered if some important work thing would come up to prevent him keeping his word. He knew that kind of thing often happened. He heard other kids at school complain all the time about one or the other of their parents having to miss stuff or cancel plans due to work commitments. David knew he was lucky by more or less having three parents. There was always enough time and attention to go round when he needed it.

"Breakfast?"

Jill was holding up the box of his favourite cereal. She gave it a shake for good measure, no doubt trying to tempt him into it.

David hook his head. "No thanks. I'm not hungry."

Jill sighed. "I suspected that would be the case. I'll let you off right now, but I will be insisting you eat something at some point. There's no point in making yourself ill, then you'll be no use at all to Billie when she comes home, and I'm sure she will soon."

"You really think so?"

"I do. I remember going through puberty and it's a tough time."

"Ugh, Mum!"

"Sorry, but it's true. It happens to us all. I bet she's just going through lots of changes and having some confusing thoughts and feelings, so took off to have some time alone to think them through. Remember Mrs. Thomson said she'd packed enough food to feed an army. Maybe she had every intention of staying away for a day or two. She didn't mention any arguments with her parents or anything?"

"No, and I'm sure she would have done if she'd had one."

"What about problems at school?"

"She's not bullied if that's what you're getting at. She's actually pretty popular. She isn't one of the really popular crowd, but they do like her and she hangs out with them now and again. Everyone seems to like her actually, and she's quite good at most of her subjects and isn't ever in the bad books with any of the teachers."

"Okay, I just thought I'd ask. I've got to go shopping later today so I'm going to pop over to her house and see if Mrs. Thomson would like me to pick anything up for them, or if there's anything else I can do. I know they'll want someone at the house all the time in case she comes back. Is there any message you want me to pass on?"

"Just tell Mrs. Thomson that I miss her and hope she comes home soon, and if I can help, I'll do anything."

"Okay, honey, I'll do just that," Jill said with an understanding smile. "I shouldn't be too long. Will you two be here when I get back?"

"Probably not. Andrew's going to help me look, aren't you?"

"Certainly am."

"Okay, I'll see you when you get back then. Stay safe, both of you."

The last was delivered with a pointed look at David and he knew exactly what she was referring to. With everything that had been going on, he'd barely had a chance to sort through his thoughts on the pool incident, but the one thing it had highlighted was that gates were indeed everywhere, and could be much closer than he would have ever believed if he hadn't seen it with his own eyes. One could open anywhere, at any time, and he could come across one when he least expected it. "We will," he replied, returning the look.

"So where do you want to look today," Andrew asked as Jill left them alone in the kitchen.

David frowned, thinking hard. "I'm sure if she took her backpack she must have been heading into the woods. It's the only thing that makes sense. Billie isn't a bag type of girl and normally just uses her pockets. The only time I've seen her carry one apart from school is when we're going to play in the woods. Just because she didn't go to the treehouse doesn't mean she didn't head in there. We did mention last time that we were kind of outgrowing the treehouse anyway. Maybe she went looking for a new spot."

"Okay then. I'll just go and change into my boots. That'll make trudging through the woods a bit easier. I already ruined one pair of dress shoes last night," Andrew said with a chuckle. "I'll be back in a minute. Be ready to go when I get back?"

"Yeah, I've just got to grab my..."

David didn't finish the sentence. He was up and out of his chair, tearing through the door from the kitchen that lead out into the garage to see if he could catch his mum. He was in luck. She was just climbing into her car after moving Andrew's from the driveway so she could get out. They all carried spare keys for one another's cars for times like these. Having four cars in the family could make things a little awkward, even with a double garage. "Hey Mum, will you do something for me?"

"Of course, dear, what is it?"

"Will you ask Mrs. Thomson if Billie took her compass with her when she went out?"

"Is that significant?"

"I don't know. It might be. She wasn't wearing it the other day but that might have been because we were going swimming, but maybe she only wears it when she's going somewhere she thinks she might need it. Maybe it'll give us a clue. Find out as much as you can for me?"

"Will do," Jill agreed, feeling proud that her son was still trying to think clearly and come up with things that could help despite the distress he must be in.

David watched as she reversed out of the drive, leaving Andrew's car on the street since he was about to use it anyway. He gave her the last wave before he closed the garage door behind her.

He turned to head back into the house and as he did so, something sitting beside the connecting door caught his eye. In all honesty, the combination of brilliant white, pastel pink and hot pink combined with glitter and sparkly gems couldn't have failed to jump out at him, but that wasn't what took his attention. After all, he'd seen Candy's gaudy trainers a million times. What was unusual was that they were sitting out here and if he wasn't mistaken, there were wet leaves and mud all over them.

He picked them up to inspect them more closely, quite unable to believe his eyes. Yep, they were definitely filthy and that was so not Candy. She only ever ran on the treadmill or on the pavement when it was dry, not even being able to bring herself to step in the smallest of puddles and get in the least bit wet or dirty. She adored these trainers, often going on about exactly how many crystals were painstakingly glued onto each one. Yet he couldn't deny what he was seeing, and he'd seen his own trainers and hiking boots in exactly the same condition hundreds of times. For some inexplicable reason, Candy had been in the woods recently, and judging by the mud and leaves not yet being dry, it had been *very* recently.

Could it even have been last night, he wondered, feeling a tiny prickle of fear at the thought. He'd often found the way Candy hung around him or seemed to be watching him a bit creepy or uncomfortable, but he'd never actually been afraid of her. However, the thought of her sneaking around watching him in the woods did frighten him a little. *It couldn't really be possible, could it?* When he thought about it, there hadn't been any sign of her when he'd arrived home the night before. He hadn't given it any thought until now, assuming she was in the bathroom or her room performing some beauty regime or trying on outfits for the next day.

He had no more time to ponder the issue as he heard the piercing ring of the phone from inside the house. He placed the trainers back down where he'd found them, careful to lay them as close to how he'd found them as he could. The last thing he wanted was for anyone to know that he'd seen them. Hoping and expecting the call to be word of Billie, he dashed back inside just in time to see Andrew hanging up.

"Sorry, we're going to have to postpone our search for a while. The police would like to talk to you and are sending someone over right away."

David gulped. "The police? Why do they want to talk to me?"

"They'll want to see if you can tell them anything that will help. You *are* Billie's best friend. That's not a problem, is it?"

"No, I suppose not," David said, wringing his hands.

"David, if there's anything you want to tell me, now might be a good time."

David hesitated, desperately wanting to blurt out everything about the Hoogle and the gates, hating having to keep a secret. His mum's words flooded his mind and he clamped his mouth firmly shut. She'd specifically mentioned Andrew and Candy as people not to tell. She knew he'd have the hardest time concealing things from Andrew but had gone out of her way to tell him he had to. "No, nothing. It's just that I've never had to deal with the police before. The thought makes me a bit nervous."

Andrew chuckled. "Not having any prior dealings with them is a good thing. Listen, the authority can make everyone a little nervous when you're not used to it, even when you haven't done anything wrong. It's natural to feel that way and I'm sure they'll understand. Just be honest and open, and if you don't have anything to hide and haven't done anything wrong, then always remember that the police are your friends and are on your side, okay?"

Great. That was just what he needed to hear, considering that he did have something to hide, something huge. He wished his mum were here so he could ask her advice on this situation. Maybe things would be different considering it was the police. How was he supposed to hide or keep stuff from them? Of course, there was nothing to say that Billie's disappearance was in any way connected to the gates, but what if it was? *Exactly,* he told himself. If it were, then there would be nothing the police could do. Besides, they would probably think he was a lunatic if he tried to explain it to them, have him sent to a psychiatrist for testing, and maybe even have him sectioned. No, as much as it bothered him and felt incredibly wrong, he wouldn't be able to say anything about the gates. He just had to hope that the questioning allowed him not to have to lie or if he did, by omission only. He really didn't want to have to tell an outright lie.

Chapter Twelve

Forty minutes later, David felt shaky with relief that it was all over. Most of the questions had been along similar lines to the ones his mum had asked—ones about Billie's home and school life, her other friends, her teachers. They'd also asked about the things they liked to do together and the places they liked to go. All of those questions he'd been able to answer in great detail and with total honesty. It was only their final question that had caused him to wrestle with his own conscience. That was when they'd asked if anything out of the ordinary had happened recently, or if he'd seen any strangers around the neighbourhood. He couldn't think of anything more unusual than what had been happening or think of anything stranger than the Hoogle or the creature at the pool, but of course, he couldn't tell the police that. Utterly miserable and feeling terrible, he had to say no.

He tried to tell himself that he wasn't lying, that the police meant anything unusual or strangers relating to *this* world and not the others, but he knew that was only a technicality that wouldn't really hold up under scrutiny. Now he was torn. He desperately wanted to be out there looking for Billie but he also desperately wanted to talk to his mum, to have her reassure him that he'd done the right thing and hadn't committed a crime by not telling them he was a Gatekeeper. If only he could talk to Andrew. He knew he would make him feel better if he had all the facts.

He could hear him now, chatting to the police as he escorted them to the door, thanking them for their time and effort. He always knew the right things to say, was always so calm and in charge of every situation. He wandered back through to the kitchen diner to wait for him there. He heard the front door close.

"David," he heard Andrew call.

"In here," he called back.

"You all right? Was it really hard?" Andrew asked, entering the room.

"Kind of, but I'm okay. I told them everything I could. I hope some of it helps."

Andrew closed the door, leaning back against it, his hands behind him. "Well, you can hope, but we both know it won't, don't we?"

David looked at him, confusion written all over his face. "What do you mean?"

Andrew snorted. "Don't give me that. Just days after your thirteenth birthday, your best friend disappears off the face of the Earth without a single trace. That's no coincidence, is it? You told her, didn't you?"

David was on his feet now, starting to feel scared as well as befuddled. "Told her what?"

Andrew began to advance. "About the other worlds. I've given it a lot of thought and it's the only explanation that fits. You told her all about the other worlds beyond the gates and the Realm have decided she's a risk and taken her out of the equation, or maybe someone else that knows she's a friend of a Gatekeeper got to her. Face it, she won't be coming back."

"No! I mean, what are you talking about, what gates, what worlds? You're not making any sense," David managed to stammer, shocked that Andrew seemed to know everything after all. Had he overheard some of the conversations? Was he a part of all this too?

"Don't give me that, little Gatekeeper. You're not fooling anyone. I know all about it, and what you are, which gives me the advantage because it's obvious that you're pretty much clueless," Andrew said with a chuckle. "This just couldn't be any more perfect. I've told the police that you're insistent on spending every day out in the woods hunting for Billie and no doubt, you also told them that's where you think she'll be. What better place for you to go missing too! Especially if there's a suspected child abductor loose in the area. Two kids in as many days will make sure that's what they focus their attention on."

Andrew gave David an evil grin as he removed his hands from behind his back, revealing a roll of tape in one and a wicked looking hunting knife in the other. "Which is it to be, the easy way or the hard way? Makes no odds to me. It's not like they're ever going to find a body to examine, not once I find a gate to throw you through. The only difference is whether we make a mess on Jill's favourite carpet first. I don't fancy that much as then I'll have to clean it up. Why not just save me the trouble and say you'll go along with the easy way, please, for me?"

David stared in horror at the items in Andrew's hands, his shocked and terrified brain scrambling to keep up and make sense of the situation. Andrew meant to toss him through a gate, dead or alive! "But why!"

"Enough chat," his stepfather snarled, lunging forward to grab David.

David tried to dodge around him but he was too slow, still too confused about what was going on for his reactions to be at their best. Even if they had been, he doubted they would be good enough. For all Andrew's slightly chubby bulk, he moved at lightning speed and David's lack of sportiness was no match for him. Before he knew what was happening, his hands were clasped behind his back, both his skinny wrists being held in one of Andrew's meaty hands while the other held the knife at his throat. "So which is it to be? Come quietly and at least get to experience going through a gate first, or die right here and now?"

David tried to wrench himself free, twisting and turning his body as much as he could, but he only ended up feeling the knife press harder against his throat, the steel solid and unforgiving, icy cold against his skin. He'd never been more terrified in his life. He tried to think, tried to reason it out, relying on his logic as he'd always done all his life. If he said he would go through a gate, he would buy time, maybe find a way to escape. He slumped against Andrew. "I'll come with you," he said, trying to act resigned to his fate.

He thought about making a run for it when Andrew let him go to fiddle with the roll of tape. He was still trying to decide if he would make it to the door or not when his wrists were grabbed again and bound with the thick, grey, sticky stuff. Another piece of it was clamped firmly across his mouth.

There was no escape now.

Andrew hummed as he ripped more tape from the role. "Now for the ankles."

David's feet were shoved close together and he almost lost his balance. He felt the first layer of tape encircle his ankles, binding his legs together.

Suddenly, the door burst open and Candy flew into the room. David's heart sank. He hadn't suspected a thing about Andrew but he'd certainly been suspicious of Candy. His chances was slim as it was him against two of them, there was no hope.

Andrew glanced up, surprised at the intrusion. Seeing it was just her, he smirked and bent over again to finish the job. Intent on his task, he didn't notice Candy's return sneer.

"I knew it," she hissed before leaping across the room in their direction, her face a mask of determination that David wouldn't have even guessed she was capable of.

She aimed a graceful kick at Andrew, catching him full on the chest just below his bent chin. He never saw it coming and didn't know what hit him. He flew backwards and landed on his backside, gaping up at her, open-mouthed and wheezing, one hand clutching at his chest where she'd struck him. She didn't hesitate, delivering a roundhouse kick to his jowly chops that sent him sideways. Leaping on him and straddling him, she delivered a karate chop style blow with the side of her hand to his exposed neck. Andrew went limp and slumped in a heap.

"There, that's taken care of him," Candy said, standing up and smoothing down her pink mini skirt. "Now let's get you untied."

She knelt down and tugged at the tape around his ankles. When that didn't work, she delicately tried to unpick the end.

"Gosh, this stuff is hard!" She exclaimed. "I'm going to have to get some scissors or else I'm going to break a nail."

She leapt nimbly to her feet and strolled off in search of something to assist, leaving David standing there trussed up like a Christmas turkey, breathing heavily through his nose and wondering exactly when his life had turned completely backwards and upside down.

"Blast it, why are the kitchen scissors never where they're meant to be?" Candy exclaimed, rummaging through drawers. "I'll have to get my nail scissors from my room. I think they'll be the only other ones that'll cut that stuff. I don't want to use a knife in case my hand slips."

David was too busy staring after Candy as she exited the room to hear Andrew give a small groan or see him shake his head to clear away the fogginess. He didn't see him look around, the blue eyes focusing, lighting up when they fell on David still tied up. He didn't see him grin.

The knife had fallen from Andrew's hand when Candy had delivered that first kick but it hadn't fallen far. Silently, he reached for it, another gleeful smile crossing his face as his fingers closed around it without attracting David's attention. Stealthily, he began to rise to his feet.

Once he stood up, he stepped toward David, the knife raised high. No more easy way, no more mistakes. He wanted it over fast. The Gatekeeper had to be eliminated.

At the very last moment, some tiny sound or gut feeling alerted David to danger. He peered over his shoulder, his neck twisted as far as it would go to see, his ankles and wrists still bound and making any other movement almost impossible. He saw Andrew looming over him; saw the glint of steel. Still gagged by the thick tape, he tried to call out for help but all he managed was a muffled squeak or two. Andrew's face was menacing, his grimacing smile more terrifying than anything David had ever seen in his video games. He stared at the raised knife, unable to believe that this was it, that his life was about to end.

Their gazes locked and neither took their eyes off the other as Andrew took the final few steps he would need to bring him within range to plunge the knife into David's back. The radio that Jill loved to listen to in the morning still playing, neither of them heard the connecting door to the garage open, neither of them saw Jill step into the kitchen and take in the scene with a single glance. Neither of them saw her dash into the dining area, grab the heavy glass vase filled with the fresh flowers she'd picked from the garden that morning from the centre of the table, and raise it high.

The first thing David knew about it was when the vase crashed down heavily on Andrew's head, breaking with a loud smash. Once more, the knife fell from Andrew's hand and he slumped to the floor unconscious.

Jill gave him a prod with her foot, then nodded in satisfaction when it evoked no reaction from him. "He was starting to annoy me anyway," she said.

Just then, Candy rushed back in, grinding to a halt when she saw Andrew on the floor with the flowers scattered around him and his face lying in a puddle of water. "Oh, good going, Jill."

Jill placed her hands on her hips. "I think someone, or perhaps everyone, has a lot of explaining to do."

"Probably," Candy agreed with a shrug. "But let's get Andrew tied up first. He comes round fast, just so you know."

"Hmmm, mmm, mmm," David said, hopping up and down on the spot.

Candy giggled. "Oh, all right. You tie up Andrew, Jill, and I'll untie David."

As soon as Candy removed the tape from his mouth, David looked around at them all, absolutely bewildered. "Will someone please tell me what exactly is going on before my head explodes?"

Chapter Thirteen

"Sorry, David, talking will have to wait. We have to decide what to do about *that*," Candy said, curling up her nose as she poked Andrew with the tip of her toe. "Not only does he look untidy, but he's bleeding all over the floor and it's totally grossing me out."

Jill put her hands on her hips. "*That*, as you put it, does happen to be my husband if you don't mind."

"Oops, no offence intended, but seriously? The husband that you just clobbered over the head with a really heavy vase full of chrysanthemums and roses? You must love one another so very much, right?"

"Less of your lip please, and I didn't have much choice, did I?" Jill snapped back in response to Candy's sarcasm.

"That's enough, both of you!" David cried. "Neither of you two might care, but the man lying there injured is my stepfather—the stepfather that I love very much and thought loved me in return. If I'm not mistaken, he just tried to kill me. Now, before that really sinks in and I break my heart over it, will you two please stop fighting, make whatever decision it is you need to make and tell me what this is all about?"

Jill was horrified with herself. "I'm so sorry, David. Just because I've grown up knowing of this other side and all the subterfuge and surprises it can bring, I should never forget that you've only just learned of it."

"He'd better get used to it in a hurry," Candy grumbled.

"He will, but right now, he's still ill-equipped to deal with it."

"I am in the room, you know. Don't talk about me as if I weren't here."

"Sorry, David," Jill said.

Jill crouched down and held her arms out. He wasn't too old or too big to hurry over and accept the embrace. He'd had a massive shock. Jill knew that the numbness might be the only thing helping him hold it together right now.

She hugged him close and tried to comfort him. "David, in the lives of Gatekeepers, people aren't always what they seem. Sometimes the surprises can be very happy ones and at other times, well, let's just say they can be very nasty indeed. We'll explain everything later but for now, I'm so sorry it had to be him. I know you were very fond of him."

"I thought he was fond of me, too," David said, a slight tremor in his voice and his words punctuated with a deep sniff as tears threatened.

"He probably was," Jill said. "I doubt it could have all been an act. Look, later, okay? Let us deal with things first.

Can you do that; can you be brave for me for a little while?"

David shuddered as he realised his mum was using the same tone of voice she'd used for him when he was very small. He took one final sniff and straightened his shoulders. He wasn't a baby anymore. Whatever was happening here, he would deal with it like a man. "Of course, I can," he said, injecting as much bravado as possible.

Still, he kept his eyes averted from Andrew—and the blood oozing from the back of his head and making a sticky pool around it.

Jill nodded and stood. "So, is it okay with you if I call my father? He'll know who to contact at the Realm." The question was directed towards Candy.

"Sure, whatever," Candy said with a nonchalant shrug. "Threat is neutralised, that's all I care about."

"And you did it without even breaking a sweat," Jill said sweetly as she walked over to the phone.

"I'd be more worried about a nail. That takes longer to fix."

Jill snorted and shook her head. She had a good idea who and what Candy was now, but that didn't stop her from still being the same empty-headed, vain, appearance-obsessed, attention-seeker she'd always been before. Someone had just tried to kill her son and all Candy cared about was how much damage had been done to her bright purple and silver nail polish. *That's not fair,* the voice inside Jill's head said. *She did save his life. Technically she didn't, that was you. Only because you walked in at the right time, and he was only still alive because she'd saved him moments before.* Jill shook her head to halt and clear the internal argument. At the end of the day, David was alive, Andrew wasn't a danger for the moment, and that was all that was important. David had also learned another important lesson—at least he would have once it was all explained to him. She picked up the phone and dialled.

David listened to her explaining the situation to his grandfather by using a lot of words that he didn't understand. Well, that wasn't quite true. He understood the words just fine and it was the context they were used in that was lost to him, but the outcome of the conversation seemed to reassure Jill. She hung up with an air of satisfaction. "Your grandfather's going to contact the right people at the Realm and they're coming to collect him."

"I hope they'll hurry up about it. He's starting to come round and I'm really not in the mood to listen to him whine," Candy said.

"With his mouth taped, whining will be all he's able to do," Jill said, eyeing Andrew carefully from where she stood. "You're right, though, he's coming round. Should we hear what he has to say?"

Candy shook her head. "That's a big mistake. Look how convincing he's been so far to get this close and be this big a part of your lives. There's no telling what he might persuade us to believe, even after everything we've just seen. They can be very clever."

"True."

"You do know that to me it sounds as if you two are talking in riddles," David said. "Remember I'm still waiting for someone to explain to me what's going on."

"Oh yes, sorry," Jill said. "I suppose we might as well while we're waiting."

"Is there any chance we could go to another room?" David asked. "Away from…away from…him?"

Candy and Jill glanced at one another. "Maybe you should go with David and explain," Jill said. "I'll keep an eye on Andrew."

"Nooooo, can't do that," Candy said, drawing out the word and accompanying it with a slow shake of her head. "I'm not letting him out of my sight. If he gets away on my watch, they'll subject *me* to interrogation and hold me in one of their little cells. Have you seen the state of them? They're dark and dingy and have spiders. Not to mention people will have used the cots and the bedding before, and communal showers…just urgh!" She gave a dramatic shudder.

"Maybe we should all just stick together then," Jill said with a sigh. "Can you handle that, David?"

"Yeah, I suppose so. I just won't look at him."

"Best not, he'll give you that pleading eyes look and no doubt you won't be able to resist. First, it'll be that he needs water, then that he needs to sit up to drink it, then he needs to go to the bathroom, and before you know it—"

"That's enough, Candy."

Candy huffed and pulled a nail file from her pocket, examining every nail on each hand carefully and making a tiny little motion here, another little flick there, even though the shape was already perfect. She pointedly kept her head down, having a little sulk at the sharpness of Jill's tone.

Just then, the doorbell rang and without waiting for anyone to answer, whoever it was let themselves in without any invitation. They all heard it. Candy was instantly on alert, and Jill jumped in front of David, ready to shield him from any danger. Two men in bright blue suits, black shirts, and bright yellow ties entered the room. The combination made David a little queasy, especially when he noticed they were both wearing bright red socks.

"Guild of Gatherers from the Realm. We believe you have a Seeker?"

"May I see some ID please?" Jill asked politely but firmly.

Candy sniggered. "Isn't the uniform enough? Who else would wear that, and who would wear it if they didn't *have* to?"

One of the newcomers kept his face entirely impassive, as if Candy hadn't spoken at all. The other shot her a sour look that made her chortle with glee. "Just as well there really isn't fashion police," she hissed to David, loud enough for them all to hear.

Both men reached into their jackets and Candy poised again, as if ready for a fight. It was obvious that despite her taunting, she wasn't simply going to take them at their word either. Seeing her reaction and guessing her role in all this, the two men withdrew their wallets very slowly and carefully. They opened them and showed them to Jill.

"They look genuine," Jill said, studying the information held on the cards beneath the clear plastic inside the wallets.

"Let me see," Candy said, stepping forward.

She pulled something from her pocket and held it up towards the first card, pressing a small button. David had no idea what the item was but it looked like a mini flashlight, something that you would find on a key ring. She shone it first on one card, then the other. "Yep," she said, satisfied. "They're genuine. There's a secret hologram that reacts only to this type of special light," she explained for David and Jill's benefit. She looked at the two men. "You can take him."

The men nodded and bent to hoist Andrew to his feet. He was groggy and his knees were struggling to hold him but with their firm grip under each arm, they managed to walk him out of the house, sort of anyway. It was more of a lurch and a stagger than a walk, but they got to the door and down the path regardless.

"What's going to happen to him?" David asked as he watched his stepfather being loaded into the back of a shiny black van that had mesh over the rear windows.

"They'll hold him at their secure facility until they can gather evidence and put him on trial. After that, he'll be sentenced for his crimes. Should be a cut and dried case."

"Why is it so cut and dried? Why did he try to harm me?"

Candy was suddenly more serious than David had ever seen her. There was no sign of the giggling, vain, slightly dense female that he saw on a daily basis. "Get this straight, David. He didn't try to harm you; he wanted to *kill* you. It's that simple and the sooner you come to terms with that then the less danger you'll be in. He won't be the only one."

"Only one of what!"

"I think we should start at the beginning," Jill said. "Let's all take a seat."

Once they were all settled around the table, she began to try to explain. "You heard us mention something called the Realm today? Well, they're the ones who try to document and monitor all the gates and all the activity, the ones in charge of all the Gatekeepers and everything else, the governing body as it was."

"Think of them as your bosses," Candy added. "Head office, that sort of thing."

"Yes, quite," Jill continued. "Anyway, they're made up of the elders; descendants of the very first Gatekeepers, people who used to be Gatekeepers until the next one in their family came of age to take their place, also scholars and academics, that sort of thing. Lots of wise and smart people who've been involved in this world all their lives, as have all their family before them. There are many different divisions to handle in all different aspects of things that you haven't heard about yet. You'll learn them all eventually."

"So what do the Guild of Gatherers handle?"

"Umm, well…"

"They're the clean-up crew," Candy interjected brightly. "They get rid of bodies, they take away evidence, they gather up the criminals and take them to their own secure prison. They can help make problems go away and they can help if anyone who shouldn't witness something does, or if someone somehow ends up understanding too much about the gates."

David gulped. That sounded a bit too close to what the mob had in the books he'd read for his liking; all rather sinister and menacing. "So what sort of criminals do they gather, what sort are there that can't be handled by the actual police?"

"Ones that commit crimes specifically against members of the Realm. The thing is, David, there aren't just those that desperately want to keep the gates closed, there are also some people that believe they should all be opened and kept that way. They broke away from the

Realm and formed their own organisation many decades ago."

"Why on earth would anyone think that? Haven't they seen the things that live on the other side?"

"No, not in this world, at least not anymore. Some of the original members way back when used to be Gatekeepers, but they would have all passed on by now. I don't think that skill would have transferred. It would have mutated into something more useful for their current beliefs and objectives. I don't have any basis for this, but I've always personally thought that everyone and anyone who actually went through a gate would see the reality of what lived there. Of course, I could be wrong on that, completely wrong, but I do know for certain that when things pass into our dimension, it's different. To be honest, I'm not really sure why. These are all things you'll need to ask Grandpa about, as I only know the basics. Candy, can you help?"

Candy was busy touching up her makeup, peering at herself in her compact mirror. She shrugged as she patted at her skin with a puff. "I dunno. I've never heard of a Watcher or a Seeker who can see stuff, or any member of the Realm or the Anti-realm, only the current Gatekeepers themselves."

The last part came out almost as gobbledygook as she was shaping her mouth to reapply her lipstick as she spoke. She patted it carefully with a tissue, then began to apply lip gloss, her part in the conversation over as far as she was concerned.

David looked at Jill. "Hardly any of that made sense to me."

"I think it's as much sense as we're ever going to get from her," Jill grumbled. "Okay, you now know that the body in charge call themselves 'the Realm,' as in the main realm, this dimension, the most important one, the first, and should be the only world. Well, those that want the gates opened call themselves the Anti-realm, because they want the complete opposite of what the Realm want. They are enemies of the Realm and are against everything the Realm stands for and everything the Gatekeepers work so hard to do."

"I have more questions about that but I'm with you so far. Go on."

"So as you know, the Gatekeepers come of age quite young, and we never know who is going to be one and who isn't, so we cannot prepare them in advance due to the secrecy of it all. Therefore, there is another group of people involved. These special people are called Watchers. They do exactly what their name suggests. They watch out for the Gatekeepers, keep them from harm, and protect them from danger whenever possible. One Watcher is assigned to each Gatekeeper, and keeping them alive and helping them get to where they need to be when necessary is their sole purpose."

"Are you saying what I think you're saying?"

"I would imagine so, considering how quickly you normally pick things up. Candy is your Watcher."

"Wow, no wonder she hangs around me so much! Did you and Dad know she was my Watcher? Have you always known?"

Jill shook her head. "They never reveal themselves until their Gatekeeper is in danger. I'm sure you can see why we never even suspected her," she added with a glance and an eye roll in Candy's direction.

Candy, her makeup now perfect, snapped shut her compact with a flourish and grinned at Jill, paying no attention to the fact that she'd just been insulted.

David knew exactly what Jill meant. "So what's a…what was the other thing she mentioned, a Seeker?"

"Yes, Seekers. They're the most dangerous of all the members of the Anti-realm. The whole organisation is fanatical about keeping the gates open and the Seekers also have one sole purpose, to eliminate all the Gatekeepers so that they can't do their job. They have the idea that if they can eliminate an entire generation of Gatekeepers, then it will break the pattern and no more will ever be created. Then the gates stay open forevermore. That's their dream."

"By eliminate, you mean kill, don't you?" David's voice was quiet.

Jill wanted to soften this, to make it easier for him to handle, but like Candy, she needed him to understand how serious this was. Now wasn't the time to soft soap anything. "Yes, David. The Seekers are out to kill the

Gatekeepers, and at as young an age as possible. The fewer Gatekeepers there are in the world, the less they can handle all the gates. The longer the gates are open, the more things can come through to this version of earth, and the more people can pass through to the others."

"That's one of the things I don't get. You've told me I must never, ever, ever go through a gate. I can see why and don't have any desire to go at all. What makes the Anti-realm want to, why would anyone?"

"I really don't understand that either and I certainly wouldn't want to go. I suppose it's all about exploration, discovery, pushing the boundaries. It's always been the way of mankind, hasn't it? It could even be about fame, fortune, and riches for them, or collections of the rare and exotic. Who can ever tell what the motives of people who want to put their own world in deadly peril might be?"

"They're all a bunch of nutcases if you ask me," Candy declared, finally joining in the conversation. "But we shouldn't be worrying about their motives, only their actions. They'll stop at nothing."

Jill looked at David with sympathy. "I'm sorry it had to be him. How are you feeling about that?"

David allowed himself to remember and his face fell. Up until then, he'd been concentrating on taking in all this new information, the learning soothing him and helping him to feel better. Now it all came flooding back. "Why did it have to be him, Mum? I thought he...I thought..."

"I know, love, so did I. You two were always as thick as thieves and I thought he was wonderful for you."

"You didn't suspect?"

Jill looked horrified and shamefaced at the same time. "Good heavens no! I would never have let him so close to you if I had any clue."

"That isn't the whole story, though, is it?" Candy said, folding her arms and looking smugly at Jill.

Jill shot her a sour look. She hadn't been intending to tell her son a word of a lie, but she had been hoping to skip this part today. David could be quite timid and sensitive and she was afraid he would become completely overwhelmed if he had too much to deal with at once. "I married Andrew because I loved him. I didn't have any clue what he was. That's the truth, David; I swear it. It was your dad that didn't trust him. I refused to listen to him, thought he was being utterly ridiculous when he told me I should hire an investigator to do a background check and things. He sounded completely paranoid and I thought he was simply being over-protective. There was only a fifty-fifty chance of you becoming a Gatekeeper so it seemed ludicrous that Andrew would have come into our lives for that reason just on those odds. I never believed William, but I did agree with his insistence that you and Andrew weren't ever left alone, to a point anyway. I kept to that promise as much as possible and we made sure there was always someone close to you two when you were together."

"Until last night," Candy said. "Weren't being too careful with that promise when you let Andrew know that David was alone in the woods, were you? You even sent him out there after him. You played right into his hands."

Jill's hand flew over her mouth. "Gracious me, I hadn't thought about that! I was so worried that my head was all over the place and I just wasn't thinking straight. I'm so sorry, David. I put you in great danger."

Jill was nearly hysterical. David knew he needed to be a man about this and calm her down. Sometimes it didn't matter who was the child and who was the adult, they both had to take turns at being needy or being needed. "It's okay, Mum, you weren't to know, and you thought you were doing the best thing to keep me safe. Don't give it another thought, and please don't upset yourself over it. It was mostly my fault anyway for misjudging the time."

"Lucky for the pair of you that I was there. Sometimes I think I'm the only one who has any sense around here."

David and Jill shared a look, then David remembered something that had been bothering him. "You were in the woods yesterday, weren't you?" he said, thinking about her dirty trainers in the garage.

Candy screwed up her nose. "Someone had to follow you out there and make sure you came back in one piece, although tramping around a muddy, mucky forest was my absolute worst nightmare. I don't know why they had to assign me to someone like you. I should have told them I wanted a girl, one that likes to hang around shopping centres with her friends and spend her time in salons.

159

Instead, I get a boy, and not even a normal boy that spends his time in a gym hall playing a sport or hanging out where the girls are, oh no, I have to end up with one that likes trekking for miles through the wilderness and climbing into wet, soggy trees and sitting up there for hours. I've been cold, damp, muddy, and bitten to death by insects so many times I've lost count. You have no idea the things I went through for you. I've even ended up having to read books to pass some of the time you spent in that dusty, dreary old library. I can't decide which one's worst."

She came to the end of her tirade, folding her arms and blowing her long hair off her face with a huge puff. David couldn't help it. In spite of everything, he began to laugh. The image of Candy spending as much time at the library as he did and trying to amuse herself with nothing but books was too much, as was the idea of her tripping and stumbling her way around the woods in her miniskirts or tight little shorts. The more he thought about it, the funnier it became, especially when he realised it must have been her that he'd heard behind him last night, the footsteps, the strange noises, the frustrated catlike hiss when Andrew found him. Soon, tears were streaming down his face and he had to clutch at his tummy. Jill and Candy stared at him in amazement but his laughter was infectious. They couldn't help but join in and soon they were all laughing like hyenas, an almost hysterical reaction to the fear, stress, and trauma of the day. It was silly, but it was the perfect antidote, and exactly what they needed.

Chapter Fourteen

"Can't we go back? We've been out here for hours," Candy whined as she tripped over a large branch.

The laughter of yesterday had been a very brief respite in what were very troubled times for David. Alone in his room at night, he'd finally allowed himself to cry over Andrew; the man he'd thought of and loved as a father and believed had loved him as a son in return. It was very hard to bear to think that everything had been a lie; every moment they'd spent together, every game they'd played, every talk they'd had. Now he knew it had all just been contrived to get him to trust him and be close to him so that he could have the opportunity to kill him as soon as it became clear that he was a Gatekeeper. It was a shocking and horrific realisation that hurt David deeply. He didn't have that many people in his life that he cared about and felt truly cared about him in return, and now he'd lost two of them.

When his wracking sobs had finally subsided and slowed to a hitching chest and a sniffly nose, he'd promised himself it would be the last time he would allow himself to cry over Andrew. In fact, he wouldn't even think of him as his stepfather ever again, or even Andrew.

From now on, he was going to refer to him both aloud and in his head as the Seeker, and that would be that. He wasn't even worthy of a name anymore.

Also lying in bed in the dark, hugging his pillow for comfort, he'd realised that he absolutely had to find Billie. There was no way he was letting her go. Losing her from his life would be far worse than losing Andrew. He didn't think he would fall asleep but just in case, he set his alarm nice and early. He was going to spend an entire day looking for her and he would need to be up before dawn to prepare.

When he'd crept downstairs long before the sun had even made its first hint of an appearance, he'd been shocked when he'd flicked on the kitchen light and found Candy sitting at the dining table, staring out into the garden beyond the patio doors. "What are you doing up so early?" he asked.

She didn't turn her head towards him as she answered. "I knew what you'd want to do today. I thought that since you know the truth now, it made more sense just to go with you rather than follow you in secret."

David thought she sounded wistful, as if it was somehow the end of one thing and the beginning of something new. He suddenly had a thought. "I should thank you," he said. "Everything was so strange and unexpected yesterday but you did save my life, and you've been through a lot making sure you kept me safe, so thank you…thank you for everything."

Candy finally looked at him. "It's only just begun, David. There's a long way to go yet and just for the record, this is my job. This is what I was born to do, so there's never any need to thank me for that. You're massively important and protecting you is an honour. You and your kind keep this world safe, so it's me that should be thanking you."

David didn't know whether to be more stunned that it was the most poignant and heartfelt thing that he'd ever heard Candy say, or that it was directed towards him. The serious girl sitting at the table right now in combats, hiking boots, a thick jumper, and with her hair tied into a ponytail seemed completely different from the Candy he knew. He really hadn't gotten his head around that part yet. Oh sure, her face was still perfectly made up and her nails were still long, sparkly, bedazzled talons, but she seemed so altered, not just on the outside, but on the inside too. He couldn't think of anything more to say.

At that moment, she gave him a small smile. "The lunch is already made and ready on the counter. You just have to pack it into your backpack. I'll come along, but don't expect me to carry anything heavy."

David had felt a little comforted then. That was more like the Candy he knew. To his surprise, she'd even put together a decent lunch, one worthy of a teenage boy who'd been hiking for miles and not one of her preferred low fat, low salt, no sugar, keep-her-figure-perfect diet bars or even worse, a watery, powdery-tasting shake. He'd tried one once just out of curiosity and they weren't to his liking at all. In fact, he'd thought it was revolting. It was true that Candy looked stunning and she turned heads wherever she went, but in his mind, there were limits as to what was worth certain sacrifices and what wasn't. Denying herself decent food and the fun of treats definitely went way over every limit for any reward as far as he was concerned.

So that had been how his morning had started. It had been a bit strange but then again, strange was becoming normal in his life nowadays. Now he and Candy were deep in the woods together. If someone had said that to him a week ago, he would have doubled up with laughter at the very thought.

He was using the compass he'd received from Billie for his birthday, the inscription on the back making him incredibly sad, but the solid weight of it in his hand making him feel close to her. In spite of it, he was beginning to lose his confidence in that connection. Did he really know his best friend as well as he thought he had? If he had, he would not only have a better idea of where to look for her, but he would have known immediately why she had disappeared to. He was growing increasingly irritated with himself that neither was true.

"No, we can't," he said, finally replying to Candy's pleading question about turning back. "Look at the map. We've only covered the parts I've marked on here so far. These woods are massive and we've got a long way to go."

Candy glanced at what he was showing her, a look of desperation crossing her face. "Are you sure that's right? We must have covered more than that!"

"I'm afraid not. You can go back if you like, but I need to carry on."

"Yes, I suppose you do. I can understand that, and I'm sure you can understand why I can't leave you out here alone."

David shook his head. "Not really. This was something I wanted to ask you about and I suppose now is as good a time as any. Andrew's gone and I'm not in any danger from him anymore, so why do you need to be with me so much?"

Candy giggled. "You thought it was pretty creepy didn't you, the way I was always around or seemed to be watching?"

David flushed bright red but there was no point in denying it. "Umm…sometimes, yes."

Candy giggled again. "Don't worry, I don't blame you. If the shoe was on the other foot I would have marked you down as a seriously obsessed stalker. I'm sorry if it made you uncomfortable."

"That's okay, it makes sense now, or actually, now that I think it through, it doesn't really. If no one ever knows who is going to be a Gatekeeper and who isn't, how come you showed up so long before my birthday? Wouldn't it make sense not to assign Watchers until they knew for sure?"

It was Candy's turn to blush a little. She averted her gaze from David, unable to look him in the eye. "Well, possibly, probably, and that's maybe the way it works a lot of the time."

"I get the feeling that there's a 'but' you missed out at the end of that sentence."

"Smart little guy, aren't you? Okay, look, I didn't want to tell you this so soon, and I don't even know if I'm allowed to tell you this at all, but your grandfather was one of the best Gatekeepers the Realm has ever seen. He was one of the most powerful and most instinctive. There was no way the gene could remain dormant for long. Everyone thought it would be your mum, and believe me, she was watched just as closely from early on too. We were all really disappointed when nothing happened on her birthday. Although no one can ever say for certain, the Realm was even more convinced that there was no way the gene would skip another generation and it would absolutely have to be you that would inherit the ability. They were also equally as sure that you were going to be pretty special, just like your grandfather was. I've pretty much been trained all my life to be your Watcher, and they wanted me with you as early as possible, and that was basically as soon as they thought I was ready."

"Well, that's just great," David said, kicking at the wet, fallen leaves. "No pressure then."

"Yeah, don't let the whole special thing worry you. You'll be fine. I just know you're going to be a great

Gatekeeper, and if you can't live up to your grandfather's legacy, then that doesn't matter. You just have to be you and be the best you can be."

Her words were accompanied by a reassuring smile, but David still felt the weight upon his shoulders of all these unknown people watching him and waiting for him to morph into this super-duper Gatekeeper. He doubted it would ever happen and he really hated disappointing people. Suddenly, he realised that Candy had more or less avoided his original question and wondered if this was the answer. "So back to what I was wondering about, is that it, the fact that I'm supposed to be special in some way? Why does that mean I needed protecting sooner than anyone else?"

"Oh, dear, I think I've said far too much and opened a real can of worms. I guess it all had to come out sometime, though. Let's walk while we talk. I've got the feeling that you're not going to be happy until you've marked that entire map and if I have to be out here every day until it's done, I'd rather it was over with as soon as possible."

They began to move carefully over the uneven ground, Candy paying more attention to where she was putting her feet this time. "You see, Seekers aren't like Watchers. It isn't as if they're assigned to anyone in particular. They're basically just sent out into the world with one mission only—to wipe out as many Gatekeepers as they possibly can. They do their own hunting and finding, make their own choices, sometimes just come across them by accident and grab the opportunity. I'm afraid that Andrew being gone doesn't necessarily mean you're safe now. He won't be the only Seeker you'll come across in your life. He was just the first one who figured you out. That's one of the reasons it's just not safe to tell anyone."

"Oh, I see."

They walked in silence for a while, David keeping a close eye out for any signs of recent human activity as he gave that some thought. They occasionally saw the remnants of people passing by such as discarded litter, or the odd footprint in the mud where the ground wasn't so densely covered with the springy, wet, fallen leaves. The footprints were all too big to be Billie's, and David knew she would never litter. She loved the woods too much to spoil them or harm the animals. He could easily dismiss everything he found as not being signs of Billie or clues to her whereabouts. With only a small portion of his brainpower required to concentrate on the search, the rest was thinking over what he'd just learned.

"Candy?"

"Yes?"

"If no one knows who is and who isn't going to be a Gatekeeper, and the Gatekeepers do everything in their power to keep it all secret from anyone outside of the Realm, was it just luck on Andrew's part that he met Mum? Did he actually just meet her and fall in love normally?"

Candy gave a deep sigh. "This is the part I really didn't want to get into too deeply with you. No, the chances are that it wasn't just dumb luck, although there is maybe the tiniest, teensiest, slimmest outside chance of that. It's not likely though. The problem with the expectation of being a bit special is that it creates a lot of speculation and excitement. People whisper, people talk. I suppose we should have expected that it might have come to the attention of someone outside the Realm. I think Andrew was just the first to hear about the possibility of you, and was clever enough to make sure he was around for the big day of your birthday."

"But if that's the case, then what he did to Mum was really awful. He didn't just go out with her; he *married* her. How could someone do that just for their own agenda?"

"I know it seems really awful, but Seekers *are* awful and they'll stop at nothing. That's why you need to be extra careful and always on your guard. We can expect you to come to the attention of others, although we'll do everything in our power to prevent it."

"So you're saying that I might have a higher number of Seekers after me than usual?"

"Maybe, yes. It just depends on how well we do our job and how well you manage to do yours. You can't ever speak of this, David. Will you promise me?"

"Mum said the same thing. I promise I won't. Does she know all this, too?"

"I'm quite sure she's put the pieces together by now. If she hasn't, she will soon."

"Wow," David said with a sad shake of his head. "I was too much in shock yesterday to think about it, but this must be really hard on her. I can't imagine what it would be like to find out that the person you'd chosen as a life partner, the one who you loved that much and thought loved you back the same way, was only around because they had another agenda, not to mention that it was to kill your son. How do you even start to cope with something like that?"

Candy put a reassuring hand on David's shoulder as they walked. "I'm proud of you, David. It's very mature of you to think about your mum, and love and relationships that way. I have a feeling you're going to grow up fast. To answer your question, yes, I'm afraid it will be very hard on Jill and she'll be dealing with a lot right now, but I wouldn't worry about her too much. She might not be a Gatekeeper but her family has always been part of the Realm. She knows about the life, and what it can entail. She's a strong woman, made of stern stuff and a lot tougher than she looks. She'll be okay."

"Thanks, Candy. I needed to hear that."

"I meant it."

They walked in silence again for the next half hour or so, looking out for signs that anyone had been along this way recently, and with David keeping a close eye on his map so he always knew exactly where they were. He stopped to mark another tiny section off so he knew it had already been covered.

Candy peered over his shoulder again. "I'm even more certain that this can't be right now. Your compass is broken."

"Broken? Of course, it's not..."

David stared at the instrument, unable to believe what he was seeing. The needle that had held its position of magnetic north the entire day was now spinning wildly, unable to make a decision on which direction to turn or how far. It was making full rotations one way, then only partial rotations the other. There was no pattern nor rhyme or reason to the erratic behaviour.

"What's wrong with it?" Candy asked. "Is it supposed to do that?"

"I have no idea and no, it's definitely not supposed to do that."

"Then it's an...what's that word for something out of the ordinary? It begins with an 'a'."

"An anomaly, that's it!"

"I'm not sure that it was," Candy said doubtfully. "I don't think I know that word."

"Not the word, the reason. It has to be reacting to something out of the ordinary, and what do we know that's out of the ordinary?"

Candy chewed her lip, thinking hard as if she were taking a test. "Umm..." Suddenly her face brightened. "Gates!"

"Exactly. Other than a magnetic force, it's the only thing I can think of that might make it go haywire like this. Maybe gates carry their own type of magnetic force."

"But if gates affected compasses this way, then surely someone would have figured that out before now. I mean people walk around with these things all the time, don't they? I don't mean regular people but hikers, walkers, mountain climbers, that sort of thing."

David's shoulders slumped. "I suppose you've got a point there. Maybe I'm wrong then, I just can't think of any other explanation."

"We'll take a look around, see if you can see anything, or sense anything. Watchers can't so you're on your own here."

David did as she suggested, trying to open his mind and see if he could feel anything, peering through the trees to see if he could see any strange disturbances like at the swimming pool before the gate opened fully. There was nothing. Then he noticed significant movement within the branches of one of the large old trees.

Probably just a pigeon, he told himself, *or maybe even a squirrel.* He saw the movement again and he began to doubt his assessment. He'd seen the movement of birds and other wildlife in trees before and it had always been significantly less. Whatever this was seemed to be a little bigger and heavier, or less discreet and nimble at any rate. His heart pounding in his chest, he took a few slow steps forward closer to the tree to get a better look.

Suddenly, the leaves were flung apart and a long, reptilian snout was thrust out towards him. Green snot oozed from the jaws and nose, dripping onto the branches below. Bright green eyes glowed menacingly in the dim light of the forest. David jumped and gasped, clutching at his chest and chuckling slightly as he realised it was only a Hoogle. His relief was short lived as another snout and pair of eyes appeared from between the foliage of the tree, then another, then another. He watched in amazement as more and more popped out, all of them staring at him. Stunned, he began to count but only got so far before he lost track. There were at least thirty of them in the gigantic tree that he could see so far.

Other than at his birthday dinner with his family, he'd never seen that many together. He tried to think what it could possibly mean. One thought was that it could confirm his suspicion that there was a gate nearby. Maybe the Hoogle liked to stick close to them. Maybe they were waiting for it to open so they could go home. When one of them leapt down from the tree and made its way over, he froze in position, standing facing the tree with his compass held out in front of him. He still wasn't sure if he was comfortable with them getting too close to him, no matter what anyone said about them not being dangerous. This one didn't care what David was or wasn't comfortable with. It very much had its own plan. With one push from the powerful hind legs, it leapt up into the air and landed on David's outstretched arm.

David held his breath as the talons wrapped themselves around his skinny arm, clinging on as a bird of prey might. It was heavy and he was struggling to hold his arm up, but he was also paralysed with fear, his arm muscles rigid. The Hoogle looked at the compass, then reached down to tap the glass front, cocking its head as the needle continued to jerk and spin. It looked at David and nodded sagely as if the compass' weird behaviour explained everything. It jumped back down off his arm and ran back to the tree, chattering like a chipmunk all the way.

David slumped in relief. He pulled up his sleeve to check his arm, surprised to see that although the firm grip had caused some very mild discomfort, there was no breaking of the skin or even bruising. In fact, the only thing that remained to prove to David's mind that what he'd experienced was real were pale pink marks that were already beginning to fade away. He pulled his sleeve back down, amazed that the creature had been so careful, maybe even gentle.

"David, is something wrong? Are you seeing something?"

He glanced at the tree full of dozens of pairs of eyes, then looked back at Candy. In spite of her heavy boots and combats, she still looked soft and feminine, vulnerable even. There didn't seem any point in frightening or worrying her. "Nope, I can't see or feel anything. Does it work that way anyway? Is it only open gates I can see?"

"Yeah, probably, I'm not sure. We don't get taught all the Gatekeeper secrets. With us, it's more about physical training. You should ask your grandfather next time you talk to him."

"I will," David replied, mentally adding it to the long list of questions he already had for him. It seemed to be growing by the day. "In the meantime, I'm going to walk around a bit, see if anything happens. Maybe it's a gate that's about to open and giving off some weird signals."

"We should see if the compass goes back to normal and if it does, take a note of those coordinates where it does. That way, if it's a gate, we know exactly where it is and you know where to come if anything happens."

It was a terrific idea and David could hardly believe that it had come from Candy's mouth. He wasn't used to her saying anything he considered sensible, let alone intelligent. As if his poor brain didn't have enough to cope with, he had to try to learn to accept this new Candy too.

Together they did as she'd suggested, seeing the compass settle and return to behaving the way it should when they moved a certain distance away from the area in all directions. It was both fascinating and confusing to watch.

"It just has to be a gate," David muttered, more to himself than to Candy.

If gates normally didn't register on compasses, then there had to be something different about this one, but for the life of him, he couldn't figure out what that something might be.

"If it's a gate just about to open, can you handle it?"

David looked up, seeing the nervous look on Candy's face. "Hey, why so nervous? Aren't you my trained Watcher? Your moves were pretty impressive yesterday."

"That was against a Seeker. Handling them is what I'm trained for, as well as all the normal dangers you might come across. The thing is I can't fight what I can't see. When it comes to creatures that come through the gates, we're pretty useless."

Candy looked so genuinely upset and saddened by her limitations that David immediately felt he had to comfort her, another thing that felt odd and uncomfortable to him. Candy was always so super confident that he couldn't imagine her ever having a single self-doubt. He didn't think there was anything he could say that could reassure her, but still, he had to give it a shot.

"You're not useless at all! Don't ever think that way. Now that I understand you better, I realise just how important your role in my life is. It would be over already if it wasn't for you."

It was Candy's turn to give him a hesitant smile and thank him. He nodded, embarrassed by this whole sharing thing with her. It was time to change the subject and move on. "We should carry on. All this standing around talking won't help us find Billie."

"Right. And David, One more thing, if you ever tell anyone that I was wearing combats and hiking boots, I think I'll have to kill you myself."

David didn't doubt that she would seriously consider it.

Chapter Fifteen

Going back to school without Billie had been a miserable experience for David. He'd spent the rest of his holidays alternating between spending time with his grandfather learning whatever he was willing to teach him about his new role and spending every other moment looking for or thinking about her. It had been so long now that the so-called responsible adults and authorities were beginning to lose hope and the search was winding down. She was already being pushed aside and forgotten. He'd seen enough police procedural shows to know why, but the thought infuriated him. Even if Billie had been abducted, she wasn't dead! He was sure of that. He would know. He would feel it. Of this, he was absolutely adamant. She was still out there somewhere and no matter what, he would never stop looking for her. In the meantime, the end of the October holidays meant he was forced to return to his normal daily life.

He'd known that he'd be walking to school alone but hadn't realised just how hard her absence from his side would hit him, or how miserable he would be. It was the same in assembly, and in the classes they'd shared, and the ones they'd partnered up in, and break times, lunch, and after school when there was no one to wait for and walk home with. As if that wasn't all bad enough, the other pupils were determined to make it even worse for him. David was often teased and ridiculed at school for a whole range of things, like his lack of fashion sense and cool clothes, his not being up to date with the latest music or television programmes, his bookishness, his willingness and eagerness to please teachers, his excellent marks in everything, the list just went on and on. The other kids had no end of material to use against him. He wouldn't have called it outright bullying before, but he was realising now that this was thanks to Billie. She was popular with everyone and as such, her being his friend had afforded him a certain level of protection. Without her to keep them in check and make them think twice, he'd suddenly become the sole focus of their mean attention. They were taking great delight in being free of their restraint and torturing him now.

To top it all off, one of his favourite teachers was absent. The class had been informed that he'd had a skiing accident over the holidays and wouldn't be back for some time. They were duly introduced to a prudish looking woman in a tweed suit and lace up shoes as his replacement. Having English with Miss Barker was nothing like having it with Mr. Lucas. He'd brought everything to life for them, making everything fun, interesting, and relevant by comparing things to modern day situations and really making them think about every sentence and word they read. He'd prepare lively essay topics and have them read their compositions out, laughing and joking along with the class as well as seriously discussing the content and context of what each pupil wrote. Miss Barker was a completely different kettle of fish. The term 'doing things by the book' came to David's mind. He had no doubt that she wouldn't waver from the strict set curriculum by even an inch, and probably hadn't for the past hundred years she'd been teaching.

Her attitude matched how David thought of her appearance, dry and sharp. He had no idea how old she actually was or of her marital status, but he thought of her as the stereotypical spinster, and not the friendly, kindly ones that sometimes appeared in the novels he read. No, she was the bitter, angry type who resented the world for whatever she'd felt life should have brought her but hadn't. She also didn't seem to like kids much, or literature, or poems. It made him think that she couldn't have found a more inappropriate profession if she'd really tried her hardest. She had to be the worst English teacher in the whole wide world.

Three days into the last term of the year, David already knew that no matter how much effort he put in, he could never like the woman. He did and would continue to do his best to respect her as a teacher, though, although she was even making that hard for him. For some reasons, she didn't seem to like David much either. He'd never had his answers in class mocked by a teacher before, nor had he ever received such low marks for anything he'd handed in. He wished Billie were around to talk it over with him. He knew that if she were, she would soon have him laughing over the whole situation and maybe even give him the courage to approach the stuffy woman and address the situation head on. That was exactly the type of thing Billie would do. As it was, he would never have the courage to do any such thing so would just have to learn to tolerate it better.

He sighed as five minutes before the lunch bell rang, Miss Barker flung his open jotter onto his desk with a sneer, the mark of fifteen out of thirty written in large numbers in red pen at the top of his essay.

"Stay behind at the bell, David. I want to see you after class."

David opened his mouth to protest but found he didn't have the bravery to make any words come out. He'd never been disliked by a teacher before, nor ever been in trouble with one. This was all new to him. He knew that just a couple of weeks ago this situation might have even made him cry at home in his room if not right here in class in front of everyone. It was an improvement he was pleased with whilst knowing he still had a long way to go in the growing up stakes. At least it was a start.

"Yes, Miss Barker," he said, having to clear his throat before he could get it out loud and clear.

Several of the kids in class sniggered, delighted to see the teacher's pet not so popular anymore. This was a dream come true for them, something they'd waited in hope to see for a long time. When the bell finally rang, they left the classroom but crowded around the open door for the ones at the front to watch, and the others to listen as best they could. They weren't going to miss this for the world.

Inside the room, Miss Barker was behind her desk and David was standing in front of it, feeling very small.

"…disappointed in your work so far. Looking over all the files, you were the one I expected great things of and you've done nothing but let me down. This particular piece you handed in was just a regurgitation of other people's thoughts, the *professional's* thoughts. There was nothing original there at all."

"That's not true! If I used anything from the research I did, I credited it and fully explained why I agreed or disagreed with what was said. That's how—"

"Silence! I will not have you back chatting me. Just for that, I'm giving you detention. When the final bell rings at the end of the day you will not be going home, you will be heading back to my office to have the pleasure of my company for another hour. Do you have any questions or have I made myself quite clear?"

David hung his head. "Quite clear, Miss Barker."

Outside in the corridor, grins were exchanged and a few of the boys high-fived one another, delighted with the outcome. Detention was a common thing for some of them, but they'd never had the pleasure of seeing the same fate befall David. The following conversation was muted but excited.

"What do you think she'll make him do, lines on the board?"

"Nah, probably sit and write his essay over again, without his entire personal library for reference."

"I reckon she'll have him scrub all the desks," another said, unable to contain his glee. "I'm glad I put a big, fresh wad of chewing gum underneath mine today."

There were more sniggers, then one boy suddenly thought of something. "Hey, I don't know how we got off with it, but none of the rest of us has detention with old Barker today. How are we going to know what she makes him do? It's not like he'd ever tell us, and it won't be half so much fun if we don't know exactly what misery she inflicts on him or what torture she puts him through. How can we torment him about it if we don't have the details?"

"Oh, I've already got that sussed out," one of the school's biggest bullies and the leader of the gang said with a nasty grin. "I don't know about the rest of you, but I plan to be right outside those windows watching. If I'd known he was going to get detention, I'd have made sure that I did too. It wouldn't have been difficult, but who'd have thought the little geek would end up there? But I want to see everything that happens so I'm going to spy. I'll maybe even pick up some tips from the old dragon."

"What if you get caught?"

"Even better, then I'll be dragged inside along with him and definitely won't miss a thing. Anyone with me?"

There were murmurs of agreement all round. No one would dare say no to Justin Watt. David's detention was going to have a lot of onlookers.

Back in the classroom, Miss Barker huffed. "Good, then get out of my sight for now and I'll see you back here after school."

David turned and left, rolling up the jotter that contained the essay he'd worked so hard on in his hand. This was so unfair.

***

When the final bell rang, David was in no hurry to pack up his books and leave the history classroom. There was no Billie waiting for him out in the corridor, no friends to walk with, no one to talk over his day with, and worst of all, he had to go back to his English classroom and spend the next hour in the company of Miss Barker. He couldn't think of anything he wanted to do less. He hoped she would give him some academic work to do. At least he could enjoy doing that so the time would fly by, and he wouldn't have any reason to talk to her. He suddenly noticed that no one else had rushed out of the classroom as they usually did either. They were all looking at him, some grinning, others nudging one another and giggling, others just staring. He realised that they were all waiting to see how he was going to handle this. He decided he couldn't possibly give them the satisfaction of letting them know this was bothering him. He squared his shoulders, packed his books away, and marched out of the classroom with determination, ignoring all those that scrambled to follow hot on his heels. He actually laughed to himself as he made his way along the corridor, knowing that he must look like a mother duck with all the little ducklings trooping along in a row behind him. He reached Miss Barker's classroom and knocked firmly on the door.

"Come."

David opened the door and walked in confidently. "Good afternoon, Miss Barker. I'm here for my detention."

Miss Barker looked up from the pile of jotters on her desk in surprise. She looked David up and down, taking in the determined stance and the proud tilt of his chin. His demeanour matched his tone. She narrowed her eyes. "Feeling happy about your detention and proud of yourself, are you?"

"No, Miss Barker, but if you feel it's fitting and that I deserve it then it has to be so, so here I am."

Miss Barker raised one eyebrow and muttered to herself. David knew he must seem like a very different boy from the one in her class a few hours ago, but he'd decided that he'd been through too much to let something like his first detention at school bother him that much. In many ways, he *was* a different boy from the one that had walked out of those school doors at the beginning of the October holidays.

"Well, close the door on all those gawkers that don't seem to have anything better to do with their time, and take your seat. Stop dillydallying around."

David did as he was asked, resisting the urge to stick out his tongue at the group of classmates that were peering in as he closed the door firmly in their faces. He heard the charge of feet barrelling down the corridor like a herd of elephants and knew that at least some of them would be rushing outside to look in the window instead. He found he no longer cared. Let them gawk if they had nothing better to do. He took his seat, placed his hands neatly on the desk in front of him, and looked at Miss Barker expectantly.

She rose from her desk, gathered up several fresh sheets of paper and a pencil and walked over to him, the only sound in the room was the squeak of her thick rubber soles on the shiny vinyl flooring. She laid the paper and pencil in front of him.

"I want you to write me a story, David, and I mean a proper story, a fiction story. I don't want an essay, or a report, or a synopsis, or a discussion. I want something that's purely from your imagination. I want to see your personality and only yours in it. I don't care what it's about as long as it's original. It can be superheroes, super villains, supernatural, paranormal, monsters, ghouls, or little green men. It could even be a love story if you like. I don't care, as long as I see good grammar, good spelling, and feel the story. Let yourself go, David, express yourself on these pages, sweep me away in the story. Just don't let me down again. Do you understand?"

"Yes, Miss Barker."

She looked at him carefully, presumably to determine if he was telling the truth or paying lip service to the correct response. Finally, she huffed and returned to her own desk.

David stared at the blank paper and chewed the end of the pencil. Her request had surprised him. He'd thought she would have him do something really boring like pulling every book and stationery supply out of the huge cupboard, dust the shelves, then put everything back in exactly where it had been before. He'd been absolutely delighted at first when he'd heard he had an academic task to do. Now he wasn't so sure.

Firstly, he wasn't sure if this actually was an academic task. Oh, he'd had to write the odd short fiction story before, but this sounded much more than that, as if Miss Barker didn't just want him to conform to the rules of the English language and prove he could use it sufficiently. Instead, it sounded as if she really wanted him to come up with something brilliant and creative, to reach down into the depths of himself and pull some wild, imaginative story out from his very core. Beads of sweat began to form on his forehead. He wasn't sure if he could do that.

He always followed a carefully worked out plan for homework, had all his research books and the internet to look things up and check facts. He needed a strategy, needed a carefully structured formula, an arc. Working any other way would be chaotic, and his brain simply wasn't equipped to deal with it. The blank sheet of paper seemed to stare at him accusingly and the ticking of the large, plain, black and white wall clock grew deafening in his ears and filled his brain, stealing any rational thoughts. *What am I going to do?* He was beginning to panic.

Then it came to him.

He already had the perfect thing to write about. Okay, it wasn't fiction, but there was no way Miss Barker would know that. He didn't need to mention Gatekeepers, or Seekers, or Watchers, or anything else. All he had to do was write a story about the Hoogles! Those ugly, creepy, little monsters were the perfect characters for a mayhem filled story that could be both scary at times and funny at others as they got up to their heinous mischief. Even if he tried to tell people that they were real – which of course he never would – they wouldn't believe him anyway. As far as Miss Barker and anyone else was concerned, they would have been created from his imagination alone. It was perfect, and exactly what his teacher seemed to want if he'd understood her correctly. Thinking over his own experiences with the Hoogle, his mind began to flood with ideas. He even had to choke back a laugh as he remembered the incident on the first day of the new term.

He thought it over now, recalling it in his mind before he tried to commit it to paper.

His alarm clock had gone off early. Being winter, it was still dark outside and his room was cold, goose bumps rising on his arm as he poked it out from beneath the warm covers to turn off the alarm. Being woken knowing he had to go to school wasn't the same anymore. It certainly wasn't half as good as knowing he could spend the day looking for Billie. Still half asleep, he'd staggered through to the main bathroom, opening the door and being surprised to be hit with the bright light already on, and a fully dressed Candy standing at the sink using the mirror to apply her makeup.

"Hey, David, morning," she'd said cheerily. "Your dad's hogging our bathroom so I just popped in here. I'll be done in like two minutes, promise."

David had been unable to answer and unable to back away, his grin spreading as he'd seen what Candy couldn't. Standing on the edge of the sink had been a Hoogle. It'd been peering into the mirror and copying all the weird faces she'd made as she opened this bit of her face wide, stretched that bit, sucked in another, and generally looked ridiculous as she contorted her face into the prime position for application of a huge range of what was to David mysterious and mystical products. It had even copied the final smack of her lips to evenly spread her lip gloss when she was done. She'd turned to smile at David. "That's me, it's all yours."

He'd nodded as behind her, the Hoogle had reached into her unzipped makeup bag and swiped a lipstick before darting off with a wink. It had kept him laughing all through his morning shower. With a small smile on his face even now, he put the pencil to the paper and began to write.

Outside, the group of boys and the handful of girls that were crowding round the window and keeping an eye on what was happening inside Miss Barker's classroom looked disappointed. "Aw, all she's getting him to do is write stuff. That's pretty boring. We should just go home."

Justin turned to glare at the boy that had spoken. "No way am I going anywhere. We've no idea what might happen yet. She might not like whatever it is she's asked him to do and then he'll be for it! If you wimps want to go home to your mummies then toddle along. I'm sure there's a glass of milk and a snack waiting for you."

Justin's mocking tone caused the others to glance at one another, afraid of being the subject of more of his ridicule and scorn. One of his posse puffed out his chest and joined in. "Hey, you babies go home if you like. I'm staying."

Only a handful had the courage to walk away, most of them were girls who didn't care so much how the school bully saw them. He usually focused his attention on the boys anyway, so they had less invested in trying to please him. The rest stayed, some of them reluctantly knowing that what Justin had said was true. Their mothers would have prepared them something nice to have when they got home to tide them over until dinner. They weren't going to tell Justin that, though. As the time went on, they only grew increasingly cold, bored, and hungry, as all they saw was Miss Barker marking jotters and David frantically scribbling over sheet after sheet of paper. He didn't even raise his head to glance in their direction once, which was no fun at all. When forty-five minutes had passed and nothing more had happened, a few more of them found the mettle to grumble and walk away. Only Justin and his most loyal gang remained.

Sitting up from his hunched over position, David raised his hand. He held it that way for a minute or two before he realised that Miss Barker wasn't going to see it, she was too intent on her task of marking. "Excuse me, Miss Barker?"

She looked up, seeing him sitting there with his arm up in the air. "What is it?"

"I've finished my fiction story and wondered if you would like me to hand it in or just leave it on the desk when I'm given permission to leave."

"Finished? Well, bring it here then, don't dawdle."

David thought she seemed unusually anxious to see it but shrugged and took it over to her. She all but snatched it out of his hand and immediately began to read. "Sit," she snapped, waving a hand at him without lifting her eyes from the first page.

David went back to his seat as quickly as possible, settling himself so he could watch anxiously as her hawk-like eyes scanned the paper, wondering if she would like his story and believe it fulfilled the criteria of the instructions she'd given him. He shifted nervously—her expression was giving nothing away. His worried fingers reached to grab for his pencil, the only thing that he'd had on the desk. He needed something to fiddle with or else he might not be able to resist leaping to his feet and demanding to know what she thought. After a few blind searches while he watched his teacher, he looked down to locate it. It was no longer there.

Immediately he looked around on the floor beneath his desk, assuming it had rolled off. He couldn't see it anywhere. With a roll of his eyes, he looked around the room, the other explanation for the missing item now a little more normal and expected to him.

There was a Hoogle.

It was sitting upright on a chair three desks to his left. As soon as it realised he'd spotted it, it pretended to write furiously on the desk with that horribly pointed claw of a finger, its face a mask of pure concentration for a few moments before it huffed in the now familiar Hoogle chuckle. When it looked back at David, all amusement had fled from its face. It looked deadly serious, maybe even angry. With such extreme features, David couldn't really tell. When it came to facial expressions, the Hoogle were very hard to read. When it slowly began to shake its head and wag that extended finger at him, he could be in no doubt that he was being reprimanded for something. Even though he was almost sure now that the Hoogle in general wouldn't harm him, it was still an uncomfortable feeling to be in their bad books. He looked away quickly, surprised to find Miss Barker had finished reading his story and was staring at him intently, an all too knowing expression on her face. He swallowed hard and wondered if he could find the nerve to ask outright what she thought.

Outside, the gang members were getting restless. "Come on, Justin, nothing's going to happen now. We might as well go."

"Hang on, look, the door's opening. Let's see who it is and what happens next first. Heck, it's Froggy Ferguson, duck everyone!"

Justin was right. Inside the classroom, a brisk knock on the door had sounded before it was opened and the head teacher stepped inside. David heard a small squeak. He whirled to look at the Hoogle. It was staring back at him with those bright green eyes opened wide as if in amazement or fear. David widened his own, questioning what its problem was. The creature gave a quick shake of the head and darted off, bolting through the door that had been left slightly ajar. David watched it go open-mouthed, snapping it closed only when he realised that if anyone had noticed his actions, they would have looked slightly odd in what everyone else would see as an empty room. Luckily, the headmaster was too busy staring at David's teacher.

Mr. Ferguson was a funny looking man with an odd-shaped bald head and slightly protruding eyeballs, which attributed for the nickname that several generations of pupils knew him by. Miss Barker gave him a disapproving look. "Can I help you, Mr. Ferguson? I'm holding a detention here."

"Yes, I heard," the head teacher said, glancing in David's direction with interest. "Not like one of our finest pupils to ever be in trouble."

"Quite," Miss Barker replied, giving away nothing and making it quite clear she didn't want to continue with this conversation.

Mr. Ferguson looked a little lost for a moment, as if not knowing what to say next, but at the same time not wanting to leave. Then his expression cleared. "I was just wondering if you were going to be much longer. Everyone else has gone for the night and I was hoping to lock up."

"Won't the cleaners be here?"

"Yes, but not until much later. They have their own set of keys and don't expect to find anyone here when they arrive."

Miss Barker pursed her lips, making her face even thinner and sharper than usual. "Just so we're clear, are you asking me to leave?"

Mr. Ferguson looked between David and the teacher. He didn't notice the eight pairs of eyes peeking over the windowsill into the room from outside. Slowly, a wicked grin began to spread over his face. "Oh no, Miss Barker, I don't want either of you to leave. I've been watching you, and I know that you know as well as I do exactly what's happening, so there's no point in pretending ignorance any longer. No doubt you've been watching and waiting as many years as I have."

"Waiting for what, exactly, Mr. Ferguson?"

"Waiting to see if this little geek was going to turn into a Gatekeeper," Mr. Ferguson said, his buggy eyes practically bulging out of his head with glee as he rubbed his hands together. "Now it's time to see how all this is going to play out. I must say, I'm rather looking forward to it."

Chapter Sixteen

"Something in particular to see here, boys?"

The sultry voice made all eight young men outside the classroom window turn. One by one, their gaze was captivated by what stood before them. Candy was standing with one hip thrust out, her hand resting on it with elbow bent. Her blonde hair was arranged in a mane of gloriousness around her beautifully contoured face, her full lips formed into a gentle smile. With absolutely no consideration for the cold weather, she was wearing a pristine white, strappy top that clung tightly to her considerable curves. The neckline was topped with lace but any sense of innocence was lost in how low it sat and how much of her perfectly tanned skin it revealed, as well as the way it strained across her chest. Her long legs were encased in black denim so tight it gave the appearance of not being material at all, but instead, spray paint made to look like fabric. From just below the knee, the jeans disappeared inside shiny, black, leather boots that ended in spiked heels and pointed toes.

"Wow," Justin said after he'd recovered from seeing the vision for the first time. "Nothing much to see here, but just tell me what it was you were hoping for and I'll make it happen."

Candy raised her eyebrows. "Very tempting, I'm sure, but what I'd like is for all of you to step aside or better yet, just turn and walk away."

"Aw, baby, you can't ask me to walk out of your life when you've just walked into mine."

Justin's attempt at flirting wasn't very good in the first place, but it was ruined even more by the fact that his breaking voice changed to a high pitched squeak by the time he reached the end of his sentence. He cleared his throat, red faced, while his friends pretended not to have noticed.

Candy was torn. She fingered the large rock she held in her hand, thinking. She could easily pitch it across their heads and not hit any of them, giving herself immediate access to the school and the very classroom David was in but if they refused to move, not only did they risk being showered with shards of glass, but also they would see far too much that would need explaining. She couldn't risk either. *Darn it,* she thought, *I don't have time for all this!* These idiots were a complication she could do without, but she had no choice but to deal with them first before she could go any further. She only hoped David could hang on until then.

"Okay then, if you children really think you're man enough for some fun with the big girls, my friends and I all used to go to this school and we thought it would be super fun to break in and have a look around, for old times' sake, you know? They're all in the gym hall right now, getting ready to have a naughty little basketball game just as soon as Froggy Ferguson leaves."

"You broke into the school while the headmaster was still on the premises?" one of the boys asked, incredulous.

Candy giggled prettily. "Well, I think it's probably more accurate to say we snuck in. There wasn't much breaking and entering required since the main door was still unlocked."

"Man, that's still brave though."

Candy blushed and waved a hand at the boy. "That or dumb," she said giggling again. "No big deal. We'll sneak back out again when the cleaners arrive later. So what do you say? We were going to play amongst ourselves, but we'd all be up for a girl against boy contest. Think you can take us? I'll warn you now, we're *very* competitive."

In that moment, none of the boys cared if they could win the game or not. All they were thinking about was hot girls in gym outfits running around on a court, and the cool factor of hanging out with girls that were obviously at least five or six years older than they were and shouldn't even be on the school premises. It was forbidden and exciting, and therefore it was irresistible.

"You bet we're in," Jason replied for them all, licking his lips.

"Well, come on then," Candy said with a wink. "Race you!"

She sprinted off at top speed, running in heels no problem for a girl like her. She only hoped this plan would work. *Please be all right, David,* she thought as she ran. *Please handle things until I can get there.*

She led them to the front door of the school, entirely unconcerned about being caught as they all raced through the corridors. There were only three people still on the premises, and they would all be thoroughly occupied right now. She skidded to a halt a couple of feet before the main gym hall doors, just past the entrances to the changing rooms.

"In you go."

The boys went through eagerly, looking around in confusion when they found the place empty and in darkness.

"Hey, there's no one in here."

"Oops," Candy said, already letting the heavy swing doors fall closed behind the boys. "My mistake!"

She looked around for something she could use to slow them down a little. She would love to drag over the heavy bench and make sure they stayed exactly where they were, but she also knew that trapping them in the gym hall carried a fire risk as well as other issues. She'd been well taught to avoid putting normal people in danger while protecting her Gatekeeper. It was only ever done if it was absolutely essential and couldn't be avoided. Instead, she chose a plant pot with a large, plastic fern in it and dragged it over, placing it in front of the doors to prevent them from opening for a short while at least. The pot wasn't that heavy and if they all combined their strength, they could shift it bit by bit from the other side. Still, it would prevent them from following her immediately, and hopefully the warren of corridors and different sections of the modern comprehensive would do the rest. Ignoring the angry yells from inside the gym hall, she bolted, heading for David and hoping she was in time.

***

Back in the classroom, some things were dawning on David. Just a week or two ago, Mr. Ferguson's words would have confused and befuddled him, but after hearing Andrew talk in similar riddles, it only took him a few seconds to work out what might be going on here, and he didn't like the sound of it one little bit. Suddenly, the Hoogle squeaking in fear and bolting from the room made sense. He realised he'd learned something new about them. They loved mischief and mayhem, but obviously only liked to be in amongst the mischief and mayhem that they created themselves. They weren't nearly so keen on anything that they weren't in control of, or that might be about to get dangerous for them. David filed that knowledge away for future reference. That was the next thing dawned on him.

If he didn't find a way out of this situation, he wouldn't have a future in which to need his new information.

It sounded very much as if he was up against two Seekers here, and that scared him half to death already. He was quite sure either of them would be more than happy to finish the job.

That was when he noticed that while his brain had been using rambling, hysterical thoughts as an avoidance tactic, both his teacher and head teacher had advanced towards him. He looked frantically towards the door, wondering if his size and age would give him the advantage of speed and he could make it there if he were to simply bolt. The sea of desks in neat rows filling the room would slow him down, and there wouldn't be any way to disguise his intent, having to weave through them. Maybe if he went under...

His brain didn't give him any opportunity to contemplate or procrastinate this time. As soon as he'd had the thought, he found himself flinging off his chair, and practically diving to the floor aiming for the next desk across. He slid across the industrial grade, polished vinyl, arms outstretched in front of him as if he were trying to cut cleanly through water. Just when he thought he'd reached the dubious protection of the next desk along, his shoulder hit one of the legs, sending the desk skittering away from him and leaving him exposed. At the same time, the grey, black-speckled, anti-slip safety flooring did its job and his slide came to an abrupt halt.

He scrambled to his hands and knees and crawled as fast as he could, feeling fingers skim the back of his neck as he moved just in time. He made it to the next desk. Should he carry on, or stop and turn to put him in a better defensive position? He couldn't possibly out-crawl his opponents all the way to the door. Even with Mr. Ferguson's tall and bulky stature, he could navigate the desks quicker on his feet than David could on his hands and knees. Decision made, he flung himself over onto his backside, knees bent, his head hitting the table top as he did so, lifting it off the ground for a split second. Time stood still as he waited to see if it would tip, but it settled in more or less the same place as it had been initially, giving him some sense of cover at least. There was a rolling sound and something dropped to the floor. David didn't have time to give it any thought as in front of him, a big, leering face with buggy frog eyes appeared in front of him beneath the desk.

"Hello, David. Looks like you're trapped. Now you're mine, all mine."

***

Back in the lengthy corridors, Candy could already hear the pounding of feet behind her. She cursed the group of bullies for being in her way and slowing her down, she cursed her own failing in not assessing correctly how quickly they would move the planter from outside the door, and she cursed the fact that the sound of her own running footsteps were echoing through these empty corridors, allowing them to follow her easily no matter how light on her feet she was. It looked as if all the time she'd put into getting them out of the way had been for nothing. They were steadily gaining on her and she estimated that by the time she reached the classroom where David was, they'd be right behind her and would see everything. She would just have to worry about that later. Too much time had passed as it was so she couldn't possibly try to get them out of the way a second time. She did have some tricks up her sleeve to deal with such eventualities, but they were quite drastic and resorting to them was absolutely forbidden by the Realm unless it was completely necessary and there was no other option. With their use frowned upon by her superiors, Candy had never used them before and hadn't intended ever using them. She hoped she wouldn't have to today. She knew it would involve lengthy written reports to explain to them why she had, and if there was one thing Candy hated, it was doing any kind of written report. Once again, it was something she would have to worry about later. For now, her heart soared as she finally saw the sign that told her she'd reached the English department.

***

David placed his hands behind him and inched backwards away from that terrible smile. He'd seen one just like it before and he knew it wasn't good. It was the smile of someone who was certain they were about to get exactly what they wanted, and what they wanted was nothing but pure evil. He recognised the situation, and he also recognised that he was just as clueless as he was the first time. He had no idea what to do in these types of circumstances. He was what the bullies referred to as a nerd, a geek, as well as several other less than flattering names. He wasn't big, he wasn't strong, he wasn't athletic, he wasn't even wiry. If he was brutally honest with himself, he was a weak, skinny kid who couldn't fight his way out of a wet paper bag. He inched his way backwards, feeling a slight pain as he put his weight on his hand. He'd put it down on top of something on the floor. His fingers grabbed at it, desperately hoping it would be something useful.

"You know all I have to do is pick this desk up, don't you, David? Why don't you just stop being silly and come on out. If you do, I'll make it nice and quick. It'll be painless, David, isn't that what you want? It's much, much better than the alternative. There's always a hard way and an easy way, so are you coming out?"

"Never," David hissed defiantly. "I'll never make this any easier for you and as far as I'm concerned, there isn't any easy way to die, so I might as well make it as hard on both of us as possible."

The face disappeared and David grabbed the opportunity to glance at what was in his hand. It was the pencil that had vanished from his desk earlier. True to form, the Hoogle had taken it and moved it to another desk, the one that David was currently under and had bumped with his head. *A weapon,* he thought. It had been brand new when Miss Barker had given it to him and it still had a nice graphite point on it, even though that point wasn't as sharp as it had been. It was better than nothing.

"Do you want me to lift the desk and you grab him, or would prefer to do the lifting and let me do the honours, Miss Barker?"

David didn't wait to hear which option Miss Barker would choose. Instead, he looked at the pair of male legs that were right in his line of vision from his position beneath the desk. He leaned forward, whipped up the trouser leg of the light grey suit and with as much strength as his puny arms could muster, rammed the pencil at the fleshy part of the hairy calf, feeling a disgusting squishy sensation as it penetrated the skin and went into the fatty muscle there. His stomach lurched and he snatched his hand away, seeing the pencil stick there. He'd impaled it much further than he thought he would be able to.

Mr. Ferguson let out a piercing scream at the same time as the slightly ajar door was flung back so that it crashed against the wall. Candy, as well as her band of bully followers that arrived only seconds behind her, surveyed the scene in the room. The boys gaped, not quite able to work out what was going on, but Candy summed it up in an instant. A big man was squealing, hopping around and clutching at his calf, a hawk-like woman was standing nearby with beady eyes fixed on the man, but was making no move to help him, and wasn't currently paying any attention to David, who was scrambling backwards beneath and between desks, trying to reach the door while the man was occupied. She guessed the pencil was his handiwork and she instantly felt a flush of pride at his ingenuity and quick thinking. It also let her know exactly who the immediate threat was here. Without another moment's delay, she was in action.

With an impressive leap from a standstill, she landed on the desk closest to her and used the others as stepping stones to reach the large headmaster. Using the last desk between her and him as a makeshift springboard, she launched and twisted her body in mid-air so that she flew at Mr. Ferguson's feet first. Both her feet, booted with lethal heels, landed in the small of his back, causing him to scream even louder. The hands that had been clutching at his calf left there to ease the pain now felt elsewhere as he turned to see what had hit him. His already buggy eyes nearly popped out of his head when he saw Candy, but his surprised expression soon cleared.

"A Watcher," he practically spat.

Faced with a serious opponent, Ferguson dropped all his dramatics and put himself into the frame of mind for an actual fight. Due to his earlier pathetic antics, Candy underestimated him. His fist shot out at lightning speed and caught her firmly in the stomach, doubling her over for a second. He tried to follow up with a karate-style chop to the back of her neck but now that she had a better idea of what she was up against, she anticipated it and dropped to the ground, flattening herself against it.

Ferguson's blow hit empty air and his own forward momentum from the force he'd put behind it caused him to stumble forward. That split second advantage was all Candy needed. In a blur of blonde hair and leather boots, she was up and had leapt on Ferguson's back. Her legs were wrapped around his chest, squeezing tightly and making him pant and wheeze as she limited the oxygen he could gasp into his lungs, while her small fists rained blow after blow on the sides of his skull. She was relentless, not letting up the rhythmic and steady stream of punches for a second.

David had been watching in awe beneath the table, but all of a sudden, he felt bony fingers grip one of his shoulders. "David, get out here."

Miss Barker! In all the confusion, he'd completely forgotten about her. She was behind him, Ferguson was in front of him, and the dreaded school bullies were blocking the doorway, engrossed and amazed at the action. *What to do! Where to go!* He decided that going forward again was the safest option since Candy seemed to be handling Ferguson. The closer he was to her the better.

"David, come back here," Miss Barker called as he began crawling back into the middle of the room.

He ignored her.

Candy felt the moment her blows began to have an effect on the big man. Still on his back, she felt him beginning to stagger a little. She was making him dizzy, hopefully bringing him to the verge of passing out. She upped her efforts, pounding her fists harder and faster, squeezing her legs even tighter. Ferguson began to reel. Candy, having taken hits like this herself, knew exactly how he was feeling. His head would be spinning, his vision would be blurred with black spots growing larger and larger, and he would feel like he was on the world's most brutal funfair ride. Soon he would feel sick. It would be a toss up whether he threw up or passed out first.

David was still crawling towards Candy and had almost made it when those same claw-like lady's fingers gripped his ankles from behind. There was nothing he could do as he was dragged backwards from beneath the desk and yanked to his feet by the scruff of his neck. He was pulled backwards and her hands roughly held him by the shoulders, pinning him in place. For such an old, frail looking woman, Miss Barker had a very strong grip. David knew he was going to have to fight hard to escape.

Just at that moment, Mr. Ferguson lost his fight for consciousness. The bulky, weighty man swayed dramatically once, then twice, then toppled, falling forward. The added weight of Candy still on his back sped up his descent as the two of them hurtled towards the ground. The wooden desk that might have broken the freefall for a lesser weight at a slower speed stood no chance. It shattered into smithereens with impact, and the headmaster landed face first on the floor among the shards and splinters of the ruined piece of school furniture. Blood spurted from the nose that had made contact with first the desk, and then the ground. Candy leapt off his back as some of the blood splatter hit her pure white top, an absolutely disgusted look upon her face. She turned. "Are you okay, David?"

David realised that the hands were gone from his shoulders. He nodded mutely, unable to find his voice, wondering where Miss Barker had gone. He decided she must have known Candy would be coming for her and fled.

Then he saw that he was wrong.

Miss Barker was coming up behind Candy, the thick, wooden pointer that all teachers used when they were holding a slideshow and wanted to point to something on the screen raised above her head and poised to deliver a heavy blow.

"Candy! Look ou—"

Candy jumped as a thick, meaty hand reached out and grabbed her ankle, intent on pulling her to the floor. A fraction of a second afterwards, the stick came crashing down. To both David and Candy's surprise, it didn't hit her. Instead, it hit the only just conscious Mr. Ferguson squarely over the back of the head, sending him firmly back into oblivion.

"Blasted Seekers," Miss Barker muttered as she returned the pointer to its usual resting place and rummaged in her bottom desk drawer. "They're everywhere, and they never know when to give up."

She returned to the group, handing Candy a coil of rope. "Well, don't you want to deal with him before he comes round again? You know how persistent they always are."

"I'll do it," David said, jumping in and taking the rope.

He'd seen the glance Candy had given the rough material and then her nice, soft, perfect hands. He wanted to chuckle, thinking that they were the very hands that had been pummelling Mr. Ferguson's head relentlessly only moments ago and she hadn't given much thought to them then. Candy the warrior girl was already gone now that the danger was over, and Candy the girly girl was well and truly back. It wasn't just the transition that always dumbfounded David; it was also the speed with which it could take place. He shook his head as he hog-tied Mr. Ferguson with arms attached to ankles, something he'd seen in a movie once. Pleased with his handiwork, he stepped back to admire it some more, more for the sake of trying to gather his thoughts than anything else.

When he was ready, he addressed Miss Barker. "I'm confused. Mr. Ferguson seemed to think you were a Seeker like him, and so did I. Aren't you?"

"Not on your life! I'd never be associated with the likes of them."

"Then what exactly are you?" David asked, puzzled. "You grabbed me and held me. I thought you were going to kill me."

"Kill you? Just take a good look at the desk you were under, my lad. If I hadn't hauled you out of there, you would have been squished as flat as a pancake. Several broken bones if not just crushed to death outright. I wasn't trying to harm you; I was trying to *save* you."

"Oh, I see." David felt very small. "But then why did Mr. Ferguson think you were on his side?"

"Because that's what I wanted him to think. I recognised that slimy snake for what he was the minute I came here, which made it doubly important that I got the job. I just knew he was waiting for an opportunity to strike."

"Are you saying that the job opening here wasn't just a coincidence? You didn't...I mean Mr. Lucas wasn't deliberately..."

"Mr. Lucas is absolutely fine. He was simply persuaded to extend his skiing holiday and is probably at this minute either enjoying the slopes or sitting by a roaring fire having an après ski and toasting his good fortune. The accident was a cover story to ensure that Mr.

Ferguson didn't realise the Realm was onto him, or at least strongly suspected him, and so that the students didn't ask any awkward questions."

David rubbed his face. He was relieved that his beloved English teacher was fine, but very confused about what was going on. "Okay, so if you're not a Seeker then what exactly are you? Candy's my Watcher and I know I only have one of those."

"I'm not a Watcher either, but I used to be. I'm retired now, but I still work for the Realm in various capacities. I like to be of use wherever I can, even though I'm never kept completely in the loop with all the information anymore."

"So if you're with the Realm, how come you've been so mean to me?"

Miss Barker chuckled. "Sorry, boy, but I had to be for several reasons. Firstly, I had to let Ferguson believe I was on his side, so I had to show a severe dislike to you as part of my cover. Then I needed you to reveal yourself to me. I wanted to see if I could force your hand and trigger those Gatekeeper instincts in you by being as horrible as possible. I had to be sure you see. Secondly, when I met you, it struck me that you were still a bit on the soft side. Now don't take offence," she added seeing David's face fall. "It's time you learned not to be so sensitive. The Gatekeepers are all young, none of them has any life experience, and they often come from nice, comfortable, loving homes where the biggest worry they have is whether their mums have packed their clean gym kit for the next day. It's nothing personal. You can all be a bit soft in the beginning, and that doesn't just go for the Gatekeepers. The Watchers can be the same."

Hearing the harrumph, Miss Barker looked at Candy and gave the ghost of a smile. "Still, that wasn't too bad a job for a youngster. Could have got here a little quicker though."

"Yeah, no arguments from me there. I had some added complications I was trying to shake off first," Candy said, waving towards the group of bullies all standing just inside the door, most of them with their mouths hanging open and their eyes popping out of their heads far enough to rival Froggy Ferguson. She giggled as she looked at them.

David's eyebrows shot up in surprise. He'd completely forgotten about them. He groaned. There was no doubt that everything they'd seen and heard would be being stored away for them to use against him for the rest of the school year, making his life even more of a living hell.

"Ah, yes, Justin and his crew of idiots," Miss Barker said. "It's unfortunate that you didn't succeed in redirecting them, but no doubt you put in a decent effort. I'll likely be one of the panel reading the report. Beatrice Barker," she said, introducing herself as she held out a hand for Candy to shake.

Candy looked a little awestruck. "No way! *The* Beatrice Barker? You're a total legend! I have all your training videos and have watched them like a million times over. Candy Richardson".

"Nice to meet you, Candy. Listen, sometimes things just don't work out as planned in this world, and it seems like we have a small problem with these fools. Still, I think we have the perfect way to deal with them since it seems as if it's absolutely necessary."

Candy leapt up and down on the spot, clapping her hands together delicately with glee. "Oh goody. I've always wanted to do this but could never really justify it. Having the permission of one of the Realm's greatest ever Watchers makes it more than okay."

Suddenly, Candy's face fell as she thought of something. "Oh, but will I still need to write up that report, fill in those million forms, and go to tribunal?"

"Maybe not, not if I say I gave the order," Miss Barker said with a slightly kindlier smile this time. "Give me one moment to make the call to have that piece of slime collected and we'll get started. Just as well they're all stupid and are still standing there like ignoramuses."

"What are you two talking about?" David hissed to Candy as Miss Barker pulled a mobile phone from her handbag and talked to someone at the other end in quiet tones.

Candy grinned at him. "I told you that we Watchers can't do what Gatekeepers do, but we do have one or two impressive little tricks up our sleeves, didn't I? You wait and see."

She gave him a cheeky wink and giggled. Miss Barker returned and leant in close to Candy to whisper rapidly in her ear, causing Candy to cover her mouth with her hand as she giggled even more, nodding with delight. As Miss Barker stepped back, Candy strolled forward, swinging her hips sexily and keeping all the boys' rapt attention on her. One by one, she whispered in their ears, occasionally touching one on the forearm or the shoulder, occasionally giving a small encouraging purr. After she'd been round them all, she sauntered back over to David.

"Come on, sweetie," she said to him, bending to give him a kiss on the cheek, and putting a possessive arm around his shoulders. "You've kept me waiting long enough tonight. Time to go home, hun."

The group of bullies faces were an absolute picture as Candy and David strolled in their direction, looking for all the world like a couple, and with David not having to try that hard for her avid attention and adoration. As they reached the group, Candy reached out and gently closed Justin's agape mouth. "You'll catch flies," she said, tittering.

"And don't let me see you with such poor marks again, David," Miss Barker said sharply, coming up behind them. "And you boys, what are you doing hanging around in school after hours! Three hours detention on Saturday morning for all of you. Now get out of here, every one of you, scat, scoot. Don't you have homes to go to?"

With the fierce little teacher's attention turned on them, the boys fled, completely ignoring the no running in school rule as they charged down the corridors hoping to avoid any additions to the length of their detention.

"What was all that about," David asked once they'd gone, completely befuddled.

"We couldn't possibly let them remember hearing a conversation about Seekers, Watchers, and Gatekeepers, and we certainly couldn't let them remember seeing their headmaster attack a student," Miss Barker said. "This is a Watcher secret so don't breathe a word to anyone, but we have the ability to alter memories somewhat. It's not something we like to do and try to avoid it at all costs. Its use usually means a tribunal of sorts, and possibly a severe reprimand. However, I felt that Candy should have the chance to practice it in a real life situation under supervision, and I'll take the rap for this one."

"Thanks, Miss Barker," Candy said with genuine enthusiasm. "David, all those boys will remember is seeing you sit through a boring old detention, your headmaster coming in to say he wants to lock up, and a super-hot girlfriend coming to meet you from school who promised to kick their asses if they ever so much as looked at you the wrong way again."

David grinned at Candy. That would show those stupid bullies not to judge people by the way they looked or dressed, or even by their performance in class. It might even make them back off a little and give him some space.

As grateful as he was, he couldn't resist teasing her a little. "Umm, I hate to tell you this, Candy, but you're not as hot as you usually are right now. Your hair is sticking up all over the place, your makeup is smudged, and you've got blood all over your top."

Candy glanced down at herself and screwed up her cute little nose. "Ewwwww, I'd forgotten all about that. I need to change out of this thing. This is *disgusting.* Is my hair and makeup really that bad?"

"It's pretty bad, but it gets worse than that. I'm almost afraid to tell you this but…you've broken a nail."

The shriek that Candy let out could probably be heard at least three streets away. "I can't believe it," she wailed. "All thanks to that big fathead over there!"

She was about to march over to him and deliver a swift kick to his substantial gut with her pointed toe in retribution but Miss Barker placed a hand on her shoulder. "There's no time for any more fun and games. There was another reason I kept only David and no one else back after school today. I needed him to reveal himself to me, and fast. I was only allowed to approach him if he did so. The Realm contacted me this morning with a message. There's a massive breach in the process of opening up in the north of the country. With the Gatekeepers being so new, they're going to need every bit of help they can get. I need you to get to the train station as fast as you can. This great oaf has already detained you far too long. When you get there, go to the desk, and give this name. You'll be given tickets and more information."

Miss Barker slipped a piece of paper into David's hand. "Good luck," she said, giving them a gentle shove towards the door.

David and Candy glanced at one another and then they were off and running, heading towards their urgent assignment.

Chapter Seventeen

"Come on, I've got the car parked over here. Follow me!"

Candy was still running, her long legs eating up the ground while David ran flat out, trying to keep up with her. He'd never been much of a sprinter and was gasping for breath by the time they reached her car. He leapt into the front passenger seat while she ran to the boot. When she joined him, she was wearing a clean top, a black t-shirt this time.

"I should really learn never to wear white," she complained. "I don't think I'm ever going to get those icky stains out since I can't get it soaking in cold water straight away. I'm going to have to toss it, and it was one of my favourites too."

David wanted to remind her that they had more to worry about than a ruined top but he didn't have enough breath to talk yet and besides, she *had* just saved him yet again. When he took the time to think about it, he decided he might sound ungrateful if he said anything, so was glad he hadn't been able to blurt it out without giving it due consideration first. He tilted his head back, closed his eyes, and tried to focus on slowing his breathing down, making each inhale deeper and every exhale longer until finally, it stopped feeling like his lungs were burning and his heart was going to explode in his chest. Even once his pulse had returned to normal, he was left with a dull headache. He thought it might be the residual effect of too much adrenaline in his body. He thought he remembered reading about that in one of his books but he would need to double check just to make sure he had his facts right. Those were the types of thoughts that always preoccupied him, even more so in times of stress. Sometimes, he even irritated himself with them. He gave himself a mental shake, realising that his mind was wandering, roaming all over the place to avoid thinking about what had just happened and what might be about to happen next.

Candy glanced over at him as she drove. "You okay there?"

"I'm fine."

"You're probably just in a little bit of shock. I must admit the headmaster came as a bit of a surprise to me too. I hadn't seen that one coming, and I've known him for a lot longer than you have. I went to that school too."

David couldn't really imagine Candy at school. He looked at her, trying to picture it. He wondered what she might have looked like then but no matter how he tried to envision her – maybe chubby or super skinny, maybe really tall or really short for her age, maybe with pigtails and glasses or braces – he just couldn't do it. Candy was just Candy. His brain couldn't make sense of her looking any other way than how she did now. Not that he had any complaints on how she looked. He caught the thought and pushed it away. He definitely shouldn't ever go there; their relationship was weird enough as it was. He turned his attention back to looking out of the window. "Hey, we're going the wrong way to be going home. I thought we had to pack some stuff."

"No need. I always keep a packed bag ready in the boot of my car for the both of us. In it, you'll find clothes, toiletries, pyjamas, slippers, and a first aid kit amongst a few other bits and pieces. You just never know when you're going to need it."

"That explains the clean t-shirt then."

"Yep, see? Never know when you're going to need it. I've got an emergency nail repair kit in mine too but it'll have to wait until later. I can't do that while I'm driving. Oh, here," Candy said, suddenly thinking about something. "You'd best call Jill and tell her what's happening. She'll be worried sick already since you're so late home from school and what with Billie and everything…"

Candy didn't need to finish the sentence. David knew that every parent in the neighbourhood was on edge about the safety of their children right now, and those were the ones whose kids weren't Gatekeepers and had that as an extra concern. He took the smart phone that Candy was passing him.

"You really should think about getting one of your own now," she said. "You never know where you're going to end up or who you might need to call."

"I suppose so."

David stared at the piece of equipment in his hand, figuring out where he needed to press to bring the screen to life. It wasn't that he didn't like technology because he loved it, but he'd never really seen the point of owning a mobile phone of any type, let alone a smart phone. He wasn't into social media and only had one friend that he saw nearly every day anyway, or at least he used to. He didn't have anyone he'd want to call, text, or message in any other way, and if he wanted to play games or surf the internet then he had all his games consoles and his computer at home. If he needed to make a call, then most of the places he liked to go such as the community centre or library had payphones and they were good enough for him. The only place that didn't have one was the woods, but if he and Billie were out there exploring and having fun, he wouldn't be thinking about making phone calls anyway. The logic had always seemed sound before.

"Things are different now. You could be in danger and need help, or badly injured."

David jumped when she spoke, realising that Candy had been sending him glances from the corner of her eye, probably taking in his expressions as he examined the phone. It was almost as if she'd read his thoughts. He nodded, knowing she was right even though he still found these flashes of intuition or sensibility from Candy hard to accept.

She smiled at him. "We'll get you one when this is over. Now make that call, we'll be at the station in about fifteen minutes."

It took David most of the fifteen minutes to explain to his mum all that happened, and to calm her down afterwards. She ranted and raved about the irresponsible school board until David managed to get a word in edgeways and remind her that since they didn't know Seekers existed, they couldn't very well screen for them when interviewing for positions. Jill had to concede that he was right and that she was being irrational, although she still claimed that hearing he'd been attacked in the one place parents should be able to assume their children were safe gave her a pretty good reason to be irrational. She was much less concerned about him going to assist with the large gate that was in the process of opening, assuring him that he would do absolutely fine, that he would be of great help, and that Candy would watch his back for dangers in this world while he dealt with ones from the other. She told him to be good and to behave himself for Candy, to keep her updated whenever he found the time, and to be careful. She finished up by telling him she loved him and asking to speak to Candy. David put her on hands free so Candy didn't need to pull over.

He tuned them out as he finally allowed himself to think over what had happened at school. He was still a little stunned by it all. If he'd had to peg anyone as the bad guy, it would have been Miss Barker. She'd seemed to dislike him so much right from the start and single him out to be the object of her wrath and scorn, while Froggy Ferguson had never been anything less than jovial and convivial around him. It just went to show that what his mum, Candy, and his grandfather had been telling him was absolutely true. Seekers could be anywhere and anyone in their life. He was absolutely beginning to believe it now, but it was still a hard lesson to come to terms with and accept. By the time he'd thought it all through and made peace with it, he'd come to a conclusion.

As Candy pulled into a long stay parking space at the train station, he turned to her. "Candy, will you help me with something?"

"Sure, sweetie, if I can. What do you need?"

"Well, I think our sprint to the car told me I need to be a lot fitter so I'd like to maybe start doing some training with you on that. You know I'm not very sporty, and hiking and swimming are really the only things I'm good at, but maybe I could be better than I am now."

"Oh, that sounds like fun! I'd be like your personal trainer. Absolutely, yeah, I'm up for that. We can even shop for workout outfits together."

David grimaced but let it pass. It would be a hefty price to pay to go shopping with Candy, but if that were the trade-off for her fitness expertise then he'd have to bite the bullet on it. Besides, offering no argument to that part might soften her up for what else he needed to ask her. He braced himself and blurted it out before he lost his nerve. "And I need you to teach me how to fight."

Chapter Eighteen

"...don't really see why it would be necessary when you've got me, especially if you're training with me and could be faster and more agile. That would mean escape would be a better option than fighting, just run away. That would be much safer, and I think Jill would have my guts for garters if she found out that..."

David leant his head against the cool windowpane, staring at the ground rushing by, tuning Candy out once more. They were on the train heading for some place in the north of England whose name he couldn't remember. Ever since he'd told her what he wanted in the train station car park, Candy hadn't shut up for a second about how bad an idea it was, about how a little knowledge could be more dangerous than none at all, and how he could actually get himself hurt even more by trying to fight instead of just taking evasive action. She'd only paused when they reached the ticket counter and cited the name Miss Barker had given them. They were handed a thick envelope and two train tickets. Candy had taken the envelope from him and told him it was safer with her, and then she was back on to her constant rant, not even halting for breath to give David a chance to jump in and counter argue any of her statements. They'd found their seat on the train and she'd hooked out her nail kit before stowing their luggage, all without a single let up. She was now intent on replacing her broken nail as she spoke; using an array of instruments that David thought looked more fitting for an operating theatre or dental surgery. Whatever chemical she was using had a really strong smell too. He was surprised no one in the carriage had complained. Mind you, even if they'd wanted to they wouldn't have managed to find a break in Candy's monologue to do so, and she was far from finished yet.

"Besides, you did a pretty good job back in that classroom of keeping yourself safe until I could get there. That was some pretty nifty moves beneath the desks to keep out of his reach, and really smart thinking with the pencil too. You did great as it was. You really should leave the fighting to me. There! All done. Now I just have to let it set, then I can paint it to match the rest."

David finally had a chance to talk and he jumped in quickly before she could start again. "I understand all the points you're making but look at what happened today. You almost didn't get there in time all over some stupid school bullies. Next time, it could be something more serious that holds you up and then what do I do? I got lucky with the pencil and that was pure coincidence. It was only there because a Hoogle had taken it and put it down on another desk, one that I happened to bump my head on so it rolled off. That was all purely accidental, and if those events hadn't come together exactly as they did, I'd have been a goner."

"But the point is they did, and you took full advantage. I'm so proud of you for that."

"That isn't the point at all, though, is it? Not really."

Candy looked thoughtful as she studied the hand with the artificial nail, turning it this way and that to make sure that it matched the others in length and shape. "I'll tell you what, give me some time to think about it, okay?"

"Fair enough," David replied.

It was more than he'd hoped for after the initial flat refusal. "Umm, on that note, hadn't we better open that envelope and see if it gives us any clues as to what we might be facing when we arrive? This isn't a long journey so we should make the most of it to mentally prepare."

She waved her hand at him. "You'd better do it. My nail is going to be wet for a while and I don't want to ruin it and have to start over."

David picked up the brown, manila A4 envelope with a sense of trepidation. It was heavier than he'd expected it to be, and there was something jangling around inside. He opened it carefully and peered inside, curious and concerned at the same time. He couldn't see what the heavy thing at the bottom was so instead of reaching his hand inside, he tipped the contents of the envelope out onto the table in front of him. A set of car keys on a big rental company key ring fell out. He gave a little chuckle when he saw that it was something so innocuous, laughing at himself for expecting something sinister. He couldn't help it though. The earlier events of the day were making him feel a little jumpy and probably a little paranoid. He pulled out the two sheets of paper that still remained inside and quietly read them over.

"Well?" Candy asked the question without glancing up from the nail that she was currently painting with a bright blue polish that had a metallic sheen to it.

"Not a lot really. There's a rental agreement for a hire car in your name, and a hand written note telling us to find it in the car park of the train station, and then just a set of coordinates. That's it, no other information, no signature, nothing. You'd have thought they might have given us a bit more to go on."

"That's the Realm for you. They like to be mysterious."

She seemed so blasé about it all, but it gave David pause. "That doesn't concern you at all? It would never occur to you that we might be walking right into an elaborate trap set up by a group of Seekers?"

Candy shrugged one shoulder, blowing gently on the newly polished nail to help speed up the drying process. "Can't say it even crossed my mind."

"So now that I've pointed it out, aren't you worried?"

"There's nothing we can do about it so what's the point in worrying? As far as we know, we've received a summons from the Realm and we have to respond to that. I couldn't even imagine the punishment if we didn't obey.

We have to go, and if it turns out not to be from The Realm after all, then we'll just have to deal with that when we get there. Besides, I'm pretty sure it's all above board. After all, the message came through Beatrice Barker and everything's gone exactly as she said it would."

David felt much easier. "That's right. I forgot that you know her and can say for sure she's a Watcher and not a Seeker. You must have been thrilled when you recognised her."

Candy looked a little uncomfortable. She dabbed tentatively at her nail, checking to see if the polish was dry and avoiding David's eye as she did so. "Well, I wouldn't say I know her, just know *of* her. Her name is in all the history books and stuff. She's a total legend and was an amazing fighter. She could really kick ass."

"Okay, so you'd never met before today, but you must have recognised her from all those training videos you said you'd seen."

"Um, not really. They were made when she was in her prime, late teens, early twenties, that sort of age. It's a testament to her greatness that they're still being used to train the young Watchers today, but they were made like a hundred years ago. I didn't actually recognise her. I wouldn't really know what she looks like now. It was only the name that meant anything to me."

David let out a groan, the small comfort he'd been feeling rapidly fading. "So you can't even tell me that Miss Barker really is Beatrice Barker the legendary Watcher?

What you're actually saying is that she could be a total imposter in league with Froggy Ferguson and sending us to our deaths?"

"Well, I guess so, if you want to be that negative."

"Great. Just terrific."

David leaned back in his seat, completely exasperated. He'd just learned never to trust anyone and believe nothing, and now he was expected to take this leap of faith and trust the stranger who, when he thought about it, hadn't really stepped in that much to save him from Froggy Ferguson and had only acted at the very last minute to save him being crushed to death. Maybe that was just because they didn't want a messy body on the school premises. How was he supposed to know when to trust and when to doubt when they kept switching everything around this way? It just wasn't logical. He wasn't used to this level of chaos. Other worlds he could accept because scientifically it *kind* of made sense, but all this secrecy and subterfuge was beyond him. He fell silent, not even able to think of another word to say.

With nothing else to focus on, he simply watched Candy, amazed that she could be so calm and unconcerned about this situation. Satisfied that the coat of blue polish was now dry, she'd removed several more items from her kit and had laid them out in a neat row on the table. He looked on, both incredulous and fascinated as she applied a layer of a clear stuff that the label on the bottle said was called top coat over the nail, then very carefully took a pair of long, thin tweezers and removed a tiny, clear crystal from a small box of them, pressing it gently into the layer of clear gloop. He'd never seen such an expression of intense concentration on her face before. He imagined that a top surgeon performing the most difficult operation couldn't have concentrated any harder than Candy was on this procedure. How could she care about something so superficial at a time like this?

As if sensing his disapproving stare, she glanced up at him. "It relaxes me, okay? Make yourself useful and programme those coordinates into the GPS on my phone."

David's cheeks burned, knowing he'd been caught out judging her again. He grabbed her phone and after a few missteps, figured out how to do as she'd asked. He went on to input the train station of their destination town as their starting point for their journey. He examined the information on the screen, seeing their final destination would only be a ten-minute drive from the station where they'd be disembarking. He glanced at his watch. They were due to arrive there in fifteen minutes. He had less than half an hour before he would once again be plunged into the unknown. Deciding to take leaf out of Candy's book and distract himself with something else, he began to explore the phone, realising that in this new life it might be an invaluable tool and it was high time he got to grips with one. Finding an active internet connection, he inputted the coordinates into the maps app and selected the street view option. He was disappointed to find that there wasn't that much to see.

According to the images that appeared on the screen, their location was simply an empty field left to go to grass on the outskirts of suburbia. It gave him nothing in terms of trying to imagine what he was about to be up against, but instead only served to raise another concern. What looked like a very busy main road ran along the top end of the field. He thought of a million questions on how Gatekeepers were supposed to deal with being observed by the general public. It would look pretty funny to passers-by to see a group of kids fighting an invisible something in the middle of an empty field. How could anyone explain that one away? Why did this new life always seem to have far more questions than answers?

His musings were interrupted by the slowing of the train and the announcement of the station they were approaching in a tinny voice over the speaker system. They were here.

Chapter Nineteen

The GPS system on Candy's phone announced that their destination was immediately ahead. As they pulled up in the rental car that had been waiting for them in the train station car park just as the mysterious note had said it would be, David saw that the field wasn't just an empty field any more. The photographs he'd seen on the map's street view option were obviously out of date by at least several months. The field had been cleared and levelled, and a large building was in the process of being built. David could see from the billboards dotted around the site that it was eventually going to be one of the bigger stores belonging to a huge and well-known supermarket chain. The build was in the first stages, nothing but exposed brick walls and a roof with gaps where windows and doors would eventually be. Heavy plant machinery sat around it, silent and still. A fence made up of metal mesh panels had been erected around the site and as they sat in the car in front of it, David read the large red and white sign aloud.

"'Danger. Unsafe Site. Strictly No Entry.' What do we do now then?"

"Simple," Candy replied, already removing her seat belt and opening her car door. "We move it and drive in."

David was quick to follow her. "But the fence is huge, and the sign says it's unsafe."

Candy turned to him. "You really do have a lot to learn, don't you," she said with an affectionate, if slightly patronising, smile. "First of all, this is only a six by six foot. panel. These things aren't that heavy and look, these two here aren't even clipped together, never mind padlocked. You think it was left that way by accident? Secondly, you have to remember that the Realm is a massive organisation that has been doing their job for centuries. Their aim is to close all the gates that open, and their reason for that is to keep the human race safe from those other places. They aren't going to let people come anywhere near an open one if they can help it, are they? The Realm will have shut down the site to keep everyone away, to keep them safe, as well as to protect all our secrets. The warnings are for the normal, not for us."

"But the site doesn't belong to them, and the company must be losing tons of money with this all just sitting here so how would they manage that?"

Candy wrapped her hands around the outside bar of the fence and lifted it slightly.

She continued talking as she carried it with ease, swinging it open like a large gate. "Maybe a fake building inspector to deem the foundations structurally unsound, maybe an environmental officer saying there are underground gases or tremors or something. Really I've got no idea, but you can bet that whatever it was, they did it fast and they did it efficiently. That's what they do. Best to leave that part to them and concentrate on the part we play. Right, that's wide enough. I'll drive through; you close it behind me then jump in."

David wasn't sure that he could but Candy didn't leave him any option. Once the car had passed through, he ran to the fencing panel and gripped it in the same way she had, surprised to find that she was right; it really was quite easy to move. He put it back in place and jumped in the car. He'd barely shut the door when Candy floored the pedal and they sped towards the abandoned construction, the cheerful signs of the major chain advertising that they would be opening soon only serving to make it look more forlorn.

"Do you think there's anyone else here?" David asked. "It looks deserted."

"We'll probably find that any vehicles are round back, maybe in what's to be a loading bay or something. Perfect to make sure they aren't seen from the road and that the place doesn't attract any unwanted attention."

David was blown away when Candy was proven right yet again. How could someone who was usually so ditzy be so smart in these types of situations? As they rounded the building to the side that faced away from that main road, he saw that a whole load of cars were already parked inside the space that would eventually have large rollers doors and storage bays. Candy pulled up alongside them and leapt out. Once again, David followed.

She looked around. "I wonder where we go."

"This is the very far side of the building and there's no activity here, so I suppose we go through this way," David said, making a dash for a wide gap that lead to what he thought might be a cold storage area in the future.

He was crossing through it when he heard shouts. "We're definitely heading in the right direction, come on, it sounds as if something's happening."

They broke into a run together and burst through another opening, halting in their tracks when they saw the size of the space in front of them. It wasn't just warehouse proportions; it was humungous. It was obviously in the first fix too, with pipework everywhere and lots of thick electrical cables encased in grey shielding dangling from the walls and ceiling. He noted that the unconnected ends of them were all covered with red tape, making him wonder if the electrics were live in order for the tradesmen to have light and to power their tools. He didn't really know why he was thinking about such things. It didn't really seem appropriate but then again, neither was Candy thinking about her nails all the time, so if his brain wanted to focus on the details of the building, he would let it. Eventually, the space would be divided up but for now, nothing but the occasional brick pillar helping to support the high roof, some tools, and some building work debris filled it—that and he could see about twenty-five people. There were a handful of adults among that number and the rest of them appeared to be kids around or close to his own age. Other than the obvious adults, the eldest kid looked to be around sixteen or so. No matter what age, they all looked very small and scared in the massive space. David didn't blame them. They were arranged in a semicircle, holding hands and staring at something in the centre of the cavernous room. He had to gather all his courage to look towards whatever it was they could see. When he did, he let out a gasp.

If he'd thought the open gate he'd seen in the ceiling of the swimming pool had been big, he'd been so very, very wrong. The pulsating light disturbance he could see in front of the semicircle now reached from floor to ceiling and covered at least half the length of the entire place. He couldn't even begin to take a guess at measurements. It was simply too much for his brain to comprehend.

"David, thank goodness you made it in time. Get over here!"

The shout broke David from his reverie. He looked in the direction the voice had come from, spotting an older man he'd never seen before in his life motioning to him. He started forward, Candy by his side.

"Not you," the man snapped. "Watchers stay back. You can't help, and we don't need the Gatekeepers distracted worrying about your safety. Over there with the rest."

David glanced to where he was pointing, seeing a huddle of people of a variety of ages standing in the corner, worriedly watching the kids in the middle. He could sense

Candy bracing herself for an argument. She couldn't see what he could see. She didn't know how urgent things were and how desperate they were about to become.

"It's okay, Candy, he's right. You do what you do really well, but this bit is what I do. Go and join the others. I'll be fine, I promise."

Candy looked at him uncertainly, chewing her bottom lip.

"Go on, scoot. Just keep an eye out for any Seekers turning up. They'd be the last thing we need, and it would be a great help knowing that we don't have to worry about that."

Candy brightened, visibly pleased that she'd been given a task that made her useful again. "You got it," she said, bending down to give David a quick hug. "Go do your stuff. Be careful, though."

"I will," he reassured her as he pulled away. "See you later."

He turned and ran over to the semicircle of kids, the man running over to join him at his side.

"Grab her hand so you can add your energy to theirs and try to focus on stopping the gate from fully forming and opening while I quickly fill you in. This has been building over the last forty hours or so. It was a mad rush to shut down the site and bring in as many Gatekeepers as we could on short notice. It's mostly been the younger ones as they're always the ones that can get away from their normal lives the easiest. Anyway, never mind that right now. The problem is that they can't work for very long. The gate's too big and too powerful. It's been draining every group. They can't get enough energy together to shut it down, only slow it down. We've exhausted everyone in the vicinity. More are coming from all over the UK, but looks like they won't get here in time to prevent the opening. I think we just have to face up to the fact that it's going to happen. It doesn't help that you're all so young and inexperienced right now. This is the very first gate for many and they don't really have the mind power down pat yet. I'm hoping that when it opens, all your instincts will really kick in and the power will increase. Right now, they're only tapping into a portion of it because they don't have the knowhow or the right incentive to access it all. I'm hoping adding you will make enough of a difference. I know you've dealt with a gate before, and on your own. Let's see if you can ramp things up enough to shut it down."

The man patted David on the back and ran off to help a young Gatekeeper that looked on the verge of fainting. He had to be removed from the line and half carried off to the side of the building where he was laid on the ground. Another adult rushed to him with a pillow, blanket, and water.

"Oh blast and bother," the girl standing next to David said. "We were hoping you'd increase the numbers, but now you'll only be taking his place so we're back to where we started."

"At least I'm fresh and not worn out," David said, trying to offer some hope.

"That's true, good point. Is this your first gate?"

"Second."

"Oh, great, you've got some experience then. That should help masses. We haven't had much time to chat but I don't think anyone else here apart from Paul over there has come across a gate yet, only the Hoogles, and they're bad enough."

"They're not so bad once you get used to them," David said with a smile, thinking about how scared he was when he first saw one. "We'd better stop chatting though and start focusing. I've got a feeling that whatever might come through a gate this size will be a whole lot worse than a pesky little Hoogle."

Whether David would have added enough mind power to the group to close the gate before it fully opened or not he would never know, he didn't have enough time to try. At that moment, the shimmering white light seemed to explode into a million pixels before his eyes. He was blinded by its brightness, and it took everything he had not to let go of his fellow Gatekeeper's hand to throw his arms up over his eyes to shield them. He tried to keep his mind concentrating on seeing it close again, to visualise the white light shrink then pop out of existence altogether, but it was impossible. The sight of it bursting open was lodged in his brain. It was all he could think about, pushing everything else aside. He hoped the other Gatekeepers were doing a better job than he was but he knew in his gut that it was already too late.

Once his brain had stopped hurting and he felt his eyes had recovered enough, he risked opening them. What he saw rendered him motionless with wonder and awe. He was literally staring into another world. Yes, he'd seen it once before, but that had been a much smaller glimpse and it was high above him, making it feel unreal and not actually connected.

This was so very different. It was right there in front of him, filling his entire range of vision. He glanced over his shoulder, taking in the grey and gloomy building around him, and then looked back at the gate. He thought his head was going to explode.

Right before his eyes, only a few steps away, was the most beautiful beach he'd ever seen in his life.

The sun was shining and he could feel the heat radiating from it, warming his body from the chill of the open building in the English winter. He could hear the small waves of the lilac ocean breaking gently on the pastel pink sand that looked so soft and inviting. Palm trees with pale yellow fronds waved gently in that warm breeze and high above, birds sang beautiful songs that were full of the joys of the day. No place in the world had ever looked so pleasing and welcoming. David was hypnotised by it.

So were the others.

As if as one they all began to walk forward, still in their semicircle and still holding hands. One step, then another, only two or three more steps away from that utter paradise, the sun feeling stronger, the sea sounding louder—

"STOP!"

David jerked awake as if from a dream as he was pushed back by rough hands. The handful of adults that had been with the Gatekeepers were spread out in front of them, doing their best to physically halt them all and break their trance.

"Snap out of it, all of you! You know you can't ever go through those gates, no matter how wonderful they look. Why do you think we try so hard to keep them closed? How many people do you think would flock to that beach? You should all know better. Now that it's fully open, it should be easier to close. Get on it. Do your jobs! Ah good, reinforcements have arrived."

The older man that had addressed David earlier ran off to greet the four new arrivals that had just walked into the area. They were being ushered towards the line when the girl next to David let out a piercing scream that echoed around the building, seeming to assault his ears from all directions. When he saw what she was screaming at, he had the urge to join her. Running across the sand towards them was the most frightening thing he'd ever seen in his life.

Since the split in the Earth had occurred around the time of the dinosaurs, David had wondered if a few of the species had survived to rule on different worlds like his mum had suggested, or even if some of the creatures that currently lived in those other worlds might still carry some of the ancient DNA from those majestic beasts that had been wiped out so dramatically. Hypothetically, thinking about it whilst lying it his bed at night, the idea seemed really cool, exciting even. What he saw now confirmed that it wasn't a hypothetical idea, but instead he'd been right and it was a reality. Only he wasn't finding the idea quite so cool and exciting now. The evidence was right in front of him, and it was downright terrifying.

The large, reptilian head with the yellow eyes with black vertical slits for pupils were scary but not that much of a surprise to David. The same went for the long face and jaw filled with razor sharp teeth, thick neck, broad shoulders, and front arms with great black claws on the ends of the three fingers on each hand. They were all classic velociraptor features that he recognised instantly from his dinosaur books and posters, as well as from a series of old classic films he loved to watch from time and time again. He doubted that there were any kids here that wouldn't see what he saw and identify with the dinosaur features. That was where the similarities ended though, and it was the rest of it that had him frozen to the spot in absolute horror.

Instead of the thick torso leading to massive thighs, powerful hind legs, and a long tail, this thing seemed to be what looked like a giant ant from the base of the neck onwards; displaying the typical ant double body that David knew from reading was the mesosoma and metasoma, with the petiole dividing the mesosoma into the thorax and gaster. It had the thick, black exoskeleton that protected the body and the six legs that, in spite of the weight it had to carry, was allowing it to scuttle rapidly across the sand. The ant body was as instantly recognisable as the velociraptor parts, and it was ugly enough when looked at closely in normal size. When displayed in these giant proportions, it was absolutely hideous. The whole thing was a mutation of the most grotesque kind. Just looking at it made David feel sick, and that was before he even considered the fact that it was rushing across the sand towards the open gate.

Yet he couldn't move.

He felt as if his entire body had been dipped in liquid nitrogen. His brain was completely numb and he was absolutely frozen to the spot. He wondered whether if he tried to move he would simply snap apart like a delicate icicle. Before he knew what was happening, he could see another of the monstrous things, then another, then another.

Suddenly the frontrunner burst through the gate, letting out a terrible roar as it leapt through into their world. It was right in front of them, looking even more impossible as it stood in the empty shell of the building; it's keen, intelligent eyes taking in its surroundings. It almost seemed to smile as it gazed down upon the row of kids only a few feet in front of it. David imagined that to the creature, they must look like a buffet table.

The thought broke his paralysis.

He'd no idea where he found the courage and he had no doubt that if he'd given himself time to think it over, he would have acted completely differently. Since he didn't give himself time to think about it, he broke free from the bone crushing hand grip of the girl beside him and jumped forward to stand directly in front of the creature, his only thought to save the others.

With every fibre of his being, he concentrated on pushing the thing backwards, back into its own world where it belonged. Working alone, he wasn't nearly strong enough.

The veloc-ant-iraptor thing pounced.

The next thing David knew, he was flat on his back, a terrible face dripping saliva onto his own, hot, fetid breath making him gag. He struggled hard but was pinned to the ground in so many places by the six insect legs that freeing himself was impossible.

He was done for.

He turned his head to the side, not wanting to see that jaw as it opened wide to bite his head off as if he was its version of a jelly baby. Everything seemed to be chaotic around him; he couldn't make any sense of the shouts or the screams that echoed through the building. All he knew was that they'd failed; *he'd* failed. The Gatekeepers hadn't closed the gate or managed to keep this danger from entering their world. Sadness and regret overwhelmed him. He realised that it would be his very last thought, his very last feelings. He believed they were fitting and well deserved.

The next thing he knew, a black streak was filling his side-on vision, flying towards him. Then a mass of blonde was barrelling into the creature's side as Candy flung herself at the monster with all the speed and force she could possibly have mustered.

The weight lifted from David as the thing was taken by surprise by the sideways attack. Both it and Candy rolled over and over, almost knocking kids down like bowling pins as they went. They screeched and screamed as they tried to jump out of the way. David scrambled to his feet, for the first time clearly seeing the absolute mayhem.

Three more of the things had come through the gate and the Watchers had been unable to stand by and see their wards being attacked, even though they couldn't see what was attacking them. They'd rushed in to the mix and were kicking and lashing out blindly, hoping to connect with whatever the threat was and do some harm. David heard the crunch of bone, looking over to see one Watcher fall to the ground with a scream as the balled fist he'd thrown a punch with connected with the exoskeleton of one of the beasts and simply shattered, unable to penetrate that thick armour. The adults in charge were trying to organise the Gatekeepers into teams to tackle each creature, screaming at them to focus on pushing them back.

He looked around for Candy, spotting her on her back, her arms wrapped around the creature's middle as far as they could go, her hands not meeting in the middle. It was on its back on top of her, trying to reach behind with its short arms, snapping all around with that vicious mouth, and kicking frantically with all six legs. He could tell by her face that she was hanging on for grim death and wouldn't be able to keep it up much longer. It must have been crushing the breath from her lungs with its size and weight. He realised that without weapons, even the skilled Watchers were no match for these things, not even if they'd had the ability to see them and weren't fighting blind. The Gatekeepers were the world's only chance. With renewed hope and grim determination, David rushed over to join the small team that had been assigned to the creature on top of Candy.

He grabbed the nearest hand and yelled, "Right, everybody, we can do this. We don't have to fight with our bodies, only our minds. We've got this. This is what we're born for, this is what we do, and we're jolly well going to do it! Focus everyone; let's send this sucker back where he belongs."

His speech and utter confidence seemed to rally the team. David felt the power rise within him and he concentrated hard on imagining it flooding down through the rest of them. He felt it hum and pulse, sent it off, felt it go, then come humming and buzzing back up towards him, magnified, amplified. He drew on all their strength while continuing to send his own flooding back down the line.

"Let it go, Candy," he yelled. "We've got it!"

Candy only hesitated for a split second, then she removed her arms, putting her life into David's hands as she gave the thing a shove to the side. It found its feet quickly and tried to swipe at her with those claws and snap at her with its massive jaws, but it was already finding itself moving backwards against its will. It let out a roar of frustration as the jaw snapped down on nothing but empty space as it continued to reverse. Seeing their efforts rewarded enthused and encouraged the team and David felt a great power surge run through them. A screech filled the room as the creature flew back through the air and through the gate, landing once again on its back in the soft sand. It kicked and scrabbled, trying to right itself. When it did, it let out one more cry before it scurried off as quickly as it could in the opposite direction, soon disappearing out of the sight of the gate.

"Right, great job everyone!" David shouted. "Split up and join another team on another beast, or the one preventing anything else from coming though. Give them your strength and belief that we can do this. This fight is far from over, but we're going to win!"

They obeyed instantly and David followed his own instructions, joining another team and making short work of sending the next creature back. He'd never felt this strong ever in his life before. It was intoxicating and empowering. His mood seemed to be infectious and one by one, the creatures were all given their marching orders and sent back through the gate. As the last one ran off and the others that had been trying to come through were discouraged by watching their pack mates flee, David gathered all the Gatekeepers into their original semicircle around the open gate.

"Okay, gang, let's shut this down," he said with a huge grin.

The others returned his smiles and got to work. Their concentration and focus was almost palpable. The air was thick with it and David felt as if he could reach out and touch it. Within less than five minutes, the massive gate that they'd failed to hold was shrinking before their very eyes and finally, the white, pulsating light met in the middle and winked out of existence as if it had never been.

The disappearance of the gate was accompanied by massive cheers from the Gatekeepers. There were lots of smiles and high fives before some of them collapsed on the ground, completely exhausted. David found he didn't feel as nearly wiped out as he had the first time, although he did feel tired and a little weak. He couldn't rest yet though— there was something massively important he had to do.

He finally found Candy sitting on the ground over at one side of the building where she'd been dragged away from the fray by the other Watchers. He nodded to the ones that had stayed with her, silently thanking them for taking her to safety, before hunkering down beside her. "Are you okay?"

"I'm fine. I think I've got a cracked rib or two but not to worry. We Watchers heal pretty fast. We have to as we don't have time to be laid up. It's another one of the little tricks we have up our sleeve. How about you, are you okay?"

"Never felt better," he replied with a smile. "Thanks to you saving my butt yet again."

Candy giggled. "Don't ever let your mother hear you using that type of language. No doubt she'd blame me for being a bad influence."

David laughed along with her, knowing that it was probably true. No matter how many times Candy saved his life, his mum still wouldn't forgive her if she thought she was teaching her son anything inappropriate.

"Well, David, it looks as if you just might live up to the Realm's expectations of you after all. I must admit I had some serious doubts when you first arrived."

Startled, David turned to see the man who had greeted him on arrival standing behind him. "Um, thank you, I think," he said, unsure if he should take that as a compliment or not.

The man gave a slight hint of a smile. "It was a very rocky start that nearly got us all killed, but you managed to pull it and everyone else together, so you did okay. You displayed some impressive raw power, but you still need a lot of work and really need to hone that focus. Still, thanks for coming. I doubt we could have saved this situation without you."

With that, the man was gone, striding off to make his way around everyone there, checking to see if any of their injuries needed urgent attention. David watched and listened, relieved to find that most of the injuries appeared to be minor. Bruises and scrapes here, a sprained ankle or black eye there. The most serious injury seemed to be the broken hand of the Watcher that had punched one of the creatures. It was deemed bad enough to need to urgent attention of a doctor and he was led off, in spite of his loud protests that he was absolutely fine and didn't need one.

"Looks like no one was that seriously hurt, although I'm sorry about your ribs."

"Could be worse," Candy replied easily. "Might be a lot worse next time. We'd best head off and get you home while you're still in one piece. This is our first outing together so I don't want to take any extra chances."

David helped Candy rise to her feet and she gingerly tested out how standing felt, grimacing as she did so. He moved alongside her, taking her arm and placing it over his shoulders, giving her his support without either of them having to say a word. Slowly, hesitantly, the two of them walked together towards the area where they'd parked the car.

"Good job out there by the way," she said, her words a little strained and breathless due to the pain she was in. "I'm really proud of you."

She bent to give him a kiss on the top of his head, wincing as she did so. David flushed bright red, embarrassed by both the compliment and the action, hoping that no one saw.

"Hey, how did you know where that creature was to save me?" He asked to change the subject in a hurry. "I thought you couldn't see them."

"We can't, but it was kind of obvious that something was on top of you. I just took a wild guess and a flying tackle."

"Luckily for me, your wild guess was spot on."

"What exactly was it I was fighting anyway?"

David shook his head. "Trust me, Candy, you don't want to know. You never, ever want to ask me that question."

She gave it some thought then nodded. "I guess I can live with not knowing."

They remained silent until they reached the hire car where David had a sudden thought. "Oh, are you going to be okay to drive?"

"Yeah, I'll be fine," Candy said, unlocking the car and lowering herself gently in behind the wheel. David hurried to leap into the passenger seat, not wanting to hold her up in case it added to her discomfort.

"The station isn't far," she continued, "and I'm sure if I rest on the journey back, I'll feel much better by the time we reach home. That's if you feel up to the travelling right now. We're taught that this kind of thing can totally exhaust or traumatise our Gatekeepers and it is pretty late. We could always get a hotel room for the night and head back tomorrow if you want to? I've got everything for an overnight stay for both of us in the holdalls in the boot."

"Nah, I'm fine," David replied, fastening his seat belt. "Besides, Mum would be frantic and I've got school in the morning."

Candy nodded and started the car, pulling out of what would be the future loading bay with care, not wanting to jerk the wheel as if the pain made her wince.

"Okay, as long as you're certain. It's been a very long day for you and an awful lot has happened."

"No, it's fine. I'd really like to get home."

"Yeah, me too."

Chapter Twenty

The rest of the car journey to the train station was carried out in silence. There didn't seem to be very much else to say, and maybe they'd both said more than enough for one day anyway. Candy only spoke once, as she pulled into the car park, close to the spot where they'd picked the car up earlier.

"I wonder what I'm supposed to do with the car. Did the note say anything?"

"It didn't mention it other than to tell us where to collect it."

"Maybe we were supposed to drive it all the way home then hand it in to the nearest office or have it picked up there."

David shook his head. "Our train tickets are returns."

"Oh, good point and well spotted. I suppose I should look for the nearest office then and hand it in there. We can always get a taxi back here if it's too far to walk."

"No, you're hurt and we're both exhausted. No specific instructions were given so we're leaving it here," David said firmly, not really sure where he was finding the authoritative tone or the nerve to even consider possibly displeasing the Realm.

"I don't want to argue as it sounds good to me, but what do I do with the keys?"

"We picked them up from the ticket office so maybe we hand them back in there?"

"No, that doesn't sound right. We can't say for sure that the person behind the desk at this end would be in the know since we were given them at the other end."

David sighed. "I'm beginning to think that maybe the Realm takes all this secrecy things just a bit too far at times. Sometimes good, clear instructions would be far easier. Maybe we should just lock the keys in the car. The rental company are bound to have a spare set."

"Yes, but then nobody would know it was here and the agreement wouldn't be signed off. It could sit here for weeks and weeks and it's my name on that document. Can you imagine the bill that it would run up? How long was the rental agreement for anyway, can you remember?"

"I can't, but I don't know why I didn't think of checking the paperwork in the first place. It might give us some clues as to what to do next."

"You didn't think of it because you're so tired, that's why."

David couldn't argue with that. His eyes were feeling gritty and his head was starting to feel as if it were filled with cotton wool. He rummaged for the envelope that he'd folded up and stuffed in his pocket. Finding it, he pulled out the required paperwork and smoothed out the creases.

"Okay, let me see. Looks like it was hired just for today and tomorrow, oh, but right here it says 'To be returned to pick up point for collection by company'. Does that tell you what you need to know?"

"I'm pretty sure it means we can get out, grab our stuff from the boot, toss the keys inside, lock it up, and walk away, thank goodness."

Both relieved, they climbed out of the car, did exactly that, then walked into the station; David insisting Candy grab a seat on a bench while he found out what time the next train that would take them home was due. He returned with the information that they only had around half an hour to wait and the train should be arriving and allowing passengers to board fairly soon.

"Would you like me to get you a magazine or something to pass the time while we're waiting?"

Candy yawned. "I think I'd be too tired to even flick through just looking at the pictures. I'm okay, thanks, but if you want to go and wander round the newsagent and look for something for yourself, I'm okay to come along."

He flopped down on the bench beside her. "Nah, can't really be bothered either."

"Going or reading?"

"Both."

Candy snorted. Neither of them had the energy or inclination to talk anymore, not even when the train arrived on the platform. They boarded almost on autopilot and took their seats in silence, both of them settling back, resting their heads, and closing their eyes, not quite asleep but in a very light doze, listening out for the station announcements along their fairly short journey.

Arriving back in their hometown, they got off the train and made their way to Candy's car, both the cold and their tiredness making them shiver.

"I wish that journey had been longer," David said. "Then we could have both had a nice, long, deep sleep without risking overshooting our stop."

"No sleeping for me when you're exposed in a public place," Candy said through a jaw splitting yawn. "I've always got to keep an eye or ear out for danger. I'm just glad that we've got our own little station out here so I don't have to drive all the way from the city centre. We'll be home in no time."

She was right. They were soon pulling up into their driveway, the large, grey Victorian house that often looked cold from the outside looking immensely welcoming tonight. It was dark out and they could see the warm light of side lamps glowing through the curtains in the sitting room, practically calling them inside. Jill and William were waiting for them just inside the door, having heard the car pull up. William wrapped Candy in his arms while Jill practically smothered David with the tightness of her hug and smothered him with kisses.

"I'm so glad to see you home safe. I've been so worried, although I know I'm going to have to get used to that. It's just that this was your first proper time and it got so late and so dark out. Anyway, what are we doing standing around in the hall. Come and sit down," she cried, ushering everyone into the warm, cosy sitting room. "What can I do, what can I make? There's a casserole keeping warm in the oven, or there are plenty of things in the fridge and freezer. What do you fancy?"

David grinned, thinking that was so like his mum, desperate to feed everyone as her way of protecting, nurturing, and showing how much she cared. The fact that she was holding back on the million questions she must have made it even more significant, proving how unselfish mums were, Jill especially. Taking her up on her offer would be the one way David knew he could make her really happy, but refusing is the one way to make her feel useless and miserable.

"You know what, Mum, I'm too tired to eat a full meal, but I'd love some hot chocolate and biscuits."

"Coming right up," Jill said. "What about you, Candy?"

"Thanks, Jill, but I'm so tired I'm just going to head straight to bed if that's okay with everyone. Before I do, I just want to say that I'll have lots to tell you in the morning, but for now, David did a fantastic job. He's going to be a very special Gatekeeper, and you should both be very, very proud of him."

"Thank you, Candy."

"You're welcome. Well, I guess this is goodnight, David. Are you certain you're okay with me going? Nothing you need to talk about or ask?"

"No, I'm fine, and everything else can wait until tomorrow. I'm just glad it's over, that's all."

"Oh, it's far from over, David. In fact, this is only the beginning."

They glanced at one another, sharing a quick grin as they thought of the adventures and dangers they might face together in the future. For the very first time, David found himself not too reluctant to embrace the idea. He was ready to take those next steps into his unknown future.